Nate

The Search

A Father's Search for a Long-Lost Daughter

Dorothy May Mercer

ISBN 13: 978-62329-073-3
ISBN 10: 1-62329-073-2

It has been more than twenty years since his newborn daughter was kidnapped out of the hospital nursery. Nate's first wife never recovered from that disaster. Even though Nate healed and made a life for himself with a new family, he has never stopped looking for his firstborn.

Since then, life has treated him well. He has no reason to complain; he works hard at a very interesting, sometimes exciting and dangerous job, and takes pride in his family. Still, he sometimes wonders what happened to Sally Miller. Where is she, and what does she look like? Is she in trouble?

As the saying goes, "Be careful what you wish for."

Cover Creator:
ProBook Premade Covers

www.premade-bookcovers.com
probook.premadecovers@gmail.com

Dedication

In honor of my grandmother, Caroline Thompson Douglas 08/27/1818 - 03/26/1904, who might have made a good special agent, but had no such opportunity, this book is dedicated to the women who have served in law enforcement, the FBI, and especially to those who have worked hard and sacrificed much to become heads of field offices and departments.

Table of Contents

[Dear Reader: If you are a fan of the McBride Novels you may have read Nate's back-story, reprinted in this prologue, in *The Arlington Alias* or in *Short & Fun Stories, Vol. 2* . If not, the entire story follows here. Hang on for the beginning of Nate's ride.]

Baby Joy

Somewhere in the Western United States

thel Goodrich, and husband Nate, had been unable to have children. After years of trying, Ethel was in her late thirties, when she finally conceived. The two of them were thrilled and could not resist telling everyone right away. Ethel was getting along beautifully with no morning sickness at all, until one day she started passing blood. Her doctor admitted her to the hospital in an attempt to stop the bleeding, but it was impossible. The baby miscarried. Ethel was heartbroken beyond comfort. Nate tried to console her, but he was suffering, too.

It was necessary to do a D & C, and during the course of this procedure, suspicious cells were discovered. A biopsy was ordered, which disclosed cancer. Fortunately, it was in an early stage. Three doctors met with the unhappy couple to discuss their options. The only way to be absolutely sure that the cancer was completely gone would be to remove all of Ethel's reproductive organs.

Ethel wept. "No, no, no," she sobbed, shaking her head. "I'll do anything, chemotherapy, or whatever, but please, don't take away my uterus."

In the end, Nate won out. He couldn't risk losing his wife. Ethel underwent the surgery.

The results were as good as could be expected, as the surgeons were ninety-nine percent certain they got all the cancer. An added bonus was they were able to save some of her eggs, for possible future fertilization with Nate's sperm.

"It can be very costly," her primary care physician told them later, "but if you and Nate consent, I can refer you to a company that will complete the lab work and freeze and store the embryos for you."

"But, I don't understand," said Ethel. "How can I carry a baby, now?"

"Well, you don't, my dear. There are women who will carry it for you. The company, and its agency, has people who contract to serve as surrogates. Once the child is delivered, it becomes yours. You are the genetic and legal parents."

Nate smiled at his wife. "Let's at least have the embryos saved. We can do that much. There will be time later to decide whether we want to go through with the rest."

And so they did.

It took the couple three long years to save up enough money for the service, by scrimping and saving every dime and borrowing all they could. They even took out a second mortgage on their house and borrowed on their life insurance policies.

They researched several agencies, consulted with an attorney, and finally selected, not the cheapest, but the one they thought was the best, the most upright, and honest and the one with the best record of results.

A surrogate mother was interviewed and selected. This particular agency believed in having the mother bond with the prospective parents, and so Ethel and Nate were able to follow and enjoy the pregnancy, step by step.

Ethel's girl-friends threw her a baby shower. The surrogate mother attended. Ethel and Nate spent weeks getting everything ready, shopping and fixing up their daughter's room.

Truthfully, the baby's prospective Aunt Cynthia had trouble not buying everything in sight. The baby would have her own nursery with all the latest brand-new paraphernalia.

Ethel spent many hours in the nursery room just playing with all the cute little girlie outfits and baby things. Cynthia made the cross-country trip, twice, to share in her sister's joyful preparations.

At last, a beautiful baby girl was born by a normal delivery. Ethel and Nate were in seventh heaven. They journeyed to the hospital where they could look at their baby. She was perfect. Their happiness knew no bounds. Grandparents came, as well, during visiting hours. None were allowed to hold her, as yet. They could pick her up and take her home in six days.

Ethel tried to stay busy during the wait. She sent out birth announcements to the newspaper and to friends and relatives. It showed the baby's picture, only hours old. She and Nate had decided on a name, Joy Alice.

The night before the big day, Ethel barely slept from excitement and Nate was almost as bad. Ethel packed everything she could possibly need to bring the baby home, a little outfit, receiving blanket, warm blanket, diapers and a changing mat. She even had a warm bottle of formula, just in case.

Nate took the day off from work, had the car washed and serviced, installed the baby's car carrier in the back seat of the car. When he brought the car around for Ethel, she was more than ready. Nate snapped a picture as she left the house and one more after he seated her in the car. What a great smile! Nate would look at it, again, month's later, and realize it was the last smiling picture he had of Ethel.

Driving to the hospital, Nate observed the speed limit and drove with as much care as if Joy Alice was already in the car. He let Ethel off at the door and drove to a nearby parking space. Ethel waited for him to join her and together they took the elevator up to the birthing floor. Leaving the elevator, they walked directly to the nursery window to look in on their baby.

She was not in her bassinet, so they assumed that the nurses were making final preparations for the baby's release to her parents.

Ethel and Nate stepped to the nurses' station.

"Hello, may I help you?" asked the duty nurse.

"Yes, please, we are here to pick up our baby girl," they both beamed.

"And your names?" asked the nurse.

"We are the Goodriches, Nate and Ethel."

The nurse silently tapped into her computer. "Goodrich, you say?"

"Yes, G-o-o-d-r-i-c-h, Goodrich, Nathan and Ethel Goodrich."

The nurse typed some more and gazed at the computer. "And the date of birth?"

"Just six days ago, the nineteenth. She was born at 7:59 P.M."

"I don't see a Goodrich. What was your doctor's name? I'll look under that."

"Dr. Yarnoka, I believe," said Nate.

"Yes, that's right," Ethel confirmed. They grinned at each other.

"Yes, he is a regular here," said the nurse. "Let me try Yarnoka... ah... here is his record. He had three deliveries that day. Reinhardt, that was a boy, then another boy. They have both been discharged. Let me see, there was one girl, seven pounds, four ounces, a good weight for a newborn girl. Let's see, she lost weight for the first three days and then she started to gain, which is good. Her mother named her Sally. I like that. Sally Miller."

Ethel wanted to scream, *Will you just shut up! Get to the point!* Instead, she tried to remain calm. "We would like to take our daughter home, now, if you please."

"Well, I don't see any Goodrich here. Let me look a day forward and back. Sometimes these records get misplaced by one day, especially if it is close to midnight."

"It wasn't close to midnight," said Nate, impatiently. "Try 7:59 P.M. There can't be many at that exact time, can there?"

"Well, there was just the one, the baby girl Sally Miller was born at the exact same time, 7:59 P.M. on the nineteenth. Are you sure your baby was born at that time?"

Ethel's body started to shake. She felt sick to her stomach.

"Are you feeling all right?" asked the nurse. "You look a little pale. It's only been six days since you delivered. Maybe you should lie down."

Nate held his wife up. "Where is Sally Miller?" he demanded.

"Why, at home, I presume. She was discharged with her mother two days ago."

Ethel crumpled in Nate's arms.

"My wife has fainted!" Nate exclaimed. "Get us some help immediately."

When Ethel woke up, she was staring at pale green curtain dividers and a white ceiling. She saw Nate standing beside her, holding her hand. She turned her head toward him and moistened her lips. He merely looked at her with tears in his eyes.

"What happened?" she asked.

"You fainted."

"I mean what happened to our Baby Joy?"

"She's g-gone. Darling, I'm so sorry."

"Gone? How can she be gone?"

"The surrogate kidnapped her."

"Oh, dear God! No. She can't do that."

"She can and she did," Nate choked.

Ethel merely stared, unable to grasp what happened.

"The police have been alerted," Nate continued, trying to stem his own tears, "but, on the phone, they were not encouraging. They will try to find her, but, even if they do, we must get a Court order to try and get her back. The laws of this state are murky on the subject. We will need to hire our own private investigator and attorney."

"What about the agency? We have a contract," she wailed.

"I called them immediately. They were very sympathetic, but they said that their hands are tied. Apparently, there is no law in this state that protects the new parents. Over the years, law enforcement has stayed out of these disputes.

"It seems, if the birth mother chooses, she can keep the baby."

"Why weren't we told?" she sobbed.

Nate had no answer. The two of them were devastated. They could only hold each other and grieve.

At length, Nate signed for Ethel's discharge. They left the hospital, in sorrow, and went home, empty and forlorn.

Together they pulled the shades in Joy's room and closed the door, permanently. Ethel cried her eyes dry that day and night. Nate comforted her as long as he could and finally fell asleep in exhaustion.

During the weeks that followed, Ethel moved through her days like a zombie. She had left her job to stay home with the baby, and now she was lost. Nate gradually recovered. He had his work to keep him engaged, and there were the police and costly lawyers, keeping him busy with attempts to recover Baby Joy. At length, he had to file suit, naming the agency and the birth mother. Nate's savings were exhausted and the bills mounted exponentially.

Ethel and Nate were barely able to communicate. He tried to bring her into the discussions over the lawsuit, but she had given up hope, entirely. Whenever he brought up the subject, her tears flowed so badly, that he could not stand it.

Nate was receiving news from his private investigator about the baby's progress, but Ethel showed no interest. Eventually, he gave up trying to talk with her about Joy or anything else.

Nate had worn out his friends at work, on the subject. As time passed, the only one who remained interested and sympathetic was his sister-in-law, Cynthia Patterson. Even Joy's grandparents were tired of listening. They urged Nate to give up the lawsuit and try again with a different surrogate. After all, there were fertilized eggs still frozen, weren't there?

Nate tried to broach that possibility with Ethel. He prevailed upon Cynthia to talk with her, too. Ethel would not hear of it. She dismissed the subject and turned away from both of them, remaining mired in her misery.

Privately, Cynthia thought that Ethel should be seeing a grief counselor. One day she broached the subject with Nate, as they were talking on the phone. He promised to discuss it with Ethel.

At first, Ethel was reluctant, but eventually she agreed to go for group therapy, if Nate would accompany her. Ethel had not left the house in all this time.

The night of their first weekly class, she panicked and braced herself at the door. She couldn't do it. Nate took her arm and gently tried to pull her hands off the door-frame. Ethel started to scream. He had to let go. "Please try," he pleaded.

She shook her head, "I c-can't!"

Nate turned away, got in the car, and went to the class, alone, where he was welcomed. The people gathered in a circle of chairs. They introduced themselves by first names only, and told briefly how they lost a child. Nate had not planned to speak, at all, but when it came around to him, the words began to flow uncontrollably. Nate realized he had found people who understood.

Nate looked forward to the group meetings. Each week he invited Ethel along. She merely shook her head, "No thank you. You go on, Nate."

In time, Nate joined with the group in a restaurant after the meetings. He became acquainted with the members. These were his friends and support group. Once, he stayed behind with two of the women. This became a weekly habit with one woman in particular. Nate hated to go home. As the nightly trysts grew later, Nate let himself into the house quietly and bedded down on the sofa.

As Nate's recovery progressed, he needed to get away from Ethel. He found more and more opportunities to stay out late. She didn't seem to notice. She sat in the same chair staring, most of the time, now. Nate had just about given up fixing her meals. Hours later, the same food remained untouched. She had stopped bathing and fixing her hair. After seeing her in the same clothes, day and night, Nate would lead her into the bedroom and help her change into fresh things.

Nate couldn't afford to hire help for Ethel. At this point he was doing the laundry, cooking and cleaning. The day came when Ethel seemed unresponsive, almost catatonic. Nate made an appointment with their family doctor. When the day arrived, he cleaned her up as best he could and carried her to the car. She said nothing and made no objection.

Nate remained in the waiting room while the doctor examined Ethel. After exhausting every magazine available, Nate went to the window and asked what was taking so long.

"I'll go and check for you," said the receptionist.

Nate waited. When she returned, she told Nate that the doctor had ordered some tests. "I think they will be finished, soon. If you'll just take a seat, someone will call you when she is ready."

After more time had passed, a nurse called, "Mr. Goodrich?"

"Yes," Nate looked up.

"The doctor will see you, now. Come with me, please." She held a clipboard in one arm and opened the door for Nate with the other. "Right this way, please."

Nate followed her down a series of corridors to the very end and into a comfortable office overlooking a small pond and garden.

"Hello, Mr. Goodrich," said the doctor. "If you will just have a seat, please."

This procedure was curious. Nate perched on the edge of a leather-bound office chair and gazed directly at the doctor. What was happening? Nate was sure that nothing could faze him, now, but his palms started to perspire.

"Nate, I've been your doctor for how many years, now? We've been through a lot, haven't we?"

Nate nodded, wishing the doctor would just say it.

"I'm sorry, but I'm afraid I have some bad news."

Nate's heart raced. He wiped his palms on his pants.

"There's no other way to say it, Nate. Your wife's cancer has returned."

Nate paled. His mouth dropped open. "Uh..." he exhaled and fell back in the chair.

The doctor waited.

Nate's brow furrowed. "But... I thought... they got it all."

"I'm sorry, Nate. A few cells escaped. With the deep depression that Ethel has experienced, her body stopped fighting."

"You mean...?"

"No one knows, but I think the cancer has metastasized."

"Spread...?"

"I'm sorry."

"But, what can we do?"

"Well, I'd like to send her to a specialist. There is always hope."

"What are the chances, doctor?"

"That is impossible to say, but I'm certain that without treatment, she doesn't have long."

Nate stared.

"Maybe a few weeks, maybe less. I can't say."

"How soon can we get in to a specialist?"

"Normally, several weeks, but I have a friend who may do us a favor."

"Call him."

"Well, I'd be happy to, but without the patient's consent..."

"What do you mean, doctor? Consent?"

"Ethel adamantly refused to go, Nate."

Nate shook his head sadly. This was the final blow. He lost his baby, his savings, now his wife.

"Do you think you could talk her into it, Nate?"

"I don't know, I doubt it."

"She wants to die, Nate."

Nate drew a deep breath. "Well... I guess I'll take her home. Go ahead and make the appointment. I'll see if I can get her there." He rose and offered a hand to the doctor, who now looked almost as defeated as Nate felt.

The doctor rose and took Nate's hand. "God bless you, son," he said.

"Thank you, doctor... for everything."

As time went on, Ethel lost all interest in life. She stopped leaving her bed. Nate could no longer care for her adequately. He called Hospice for help. A kind volunteer visited, daily at first, and then more frequently. Gently she prepared Nate for the inevitable.

Cynthia took some vacation time and flew out to be with her sister and help Nate. In the end, Ethel passed, peacefully.

Nate continued with the therapy group, for a time. They helped him through his new grief. One of the divorced women volunteered to carry one of Nate and Ethel's preserved embryos and help raise the baby herself. Nate thought long and hard about this. At last, he decided against it and ordered the eggs destroyed.

This all happened several years ago. For a while, Nate called Cynthia every week. In a way, he wondered whether he and Cynthia might get together. Gradually the calls tapered off. Nate had moved on with his life. Eventually, he met someone, and married again. The couple were happily looking forward to their second child.

Nate

The Search

Chapter 1 Today, Twenty years later.

ate shifted in his seat, trying to find some way to adjust his lanky frame into an auditorium seat made for midgets. *Dammit the aging body cannot take these interminable graduation ceremonies,* he thought, ruefully. Down below the voices droned on announcing the names as the graduates moved up and across the stage, one by one. There was no getting around it, every one of the 677 names had to be read, complete with first, middle and last, in a few cases more than three names. They were only up to the H's. Nate sighed and shifted again, accidentally bumping the neighbor's elbow. "Oops, sorry," he whispered.

The neighbor shifted out of the way, "No problem," she whispered back and smiled. "It's a long evening."

"Yeah," Nate grinned and tried to tuck his elbow in.

Nate's young daughter, Joy Goodrich, had already passed through the gauntlet, receiving her empty diploma with her left hand from the high school principal, shaking hands with the president of the school board with her right, while smiling at the camera. The actual diploma, with high honors, would come in the mail.

Nate was relieved to see her successful maneuver up and down the steps tottering on four-inch heels like a make-believe grownup playing in her mother's shoes. This was all happening too soon. *I'm not ready for this,* he thought, as his mind wandered back over the years since he held that tiny little bundle of joy in his arms for the first time. No question, at that moment he knew Joy was her name and she would live up to it. Joy had captured his heart, right from the "get-go" and never let up. Well, true, there had been a few times, when he wanted to thrash her good, but he had counted to ten and never laid a hand on her.

Nate's wife knew some of the details concerning Nate's first marriage, but never about there having been a lost baby. Somehow Nate had found it too sad to discuss. And so, when their daughter was born, Nate suggested the name Joy. Somehow it seemed fitting that God had granted him another daughter to take the place of the one he lost. Besides, the first Joy never received the name Joy Alice Goodrich. The surrogate mother named her Sally Miller. They could be anywhere in the world now.

Lately things had been a little "testy" with Joy's new boyfriend. *Don't even go there,* he thought. Nate knew he wouldn't get much sleep tonight, not until he heard Joy come in from the party. Nate had even volunteered to act as chaperone.

"Oh Daddy, please," she whined, when Nate broached the subject. "You'll just spoil our fun."

"No I won't, I promise. You won't even know I'm there," he pleaded.

She just rolled her eyes, shook her head and smiled that enigmatic smile that all women seemed to have when they are dealing with men—gently manipulating them really.

"I'll buy you that new dress you've been begging me to buy for weeks," he bargained.

"My old dress will be fine," she said, "I've only worn it once."

"Yeah, but, don't you want a new one?"

"Really, it's fine, Daddy. Besides, Jeff hasn't seen this one."

Nate gulped. Jeff. That was exactly the problem, as far as Nate was concerned. That pimply-faced brat was hanging around far too much. Nate could strangle him, every time he looked at Joy with that certain gleam in his eye. Nate could remember all too well what it was like to be eighteen. He knew exactly what Jeff was thinking, and didn't like it one bit.

I could take that pipsqueak, Jeff Rotten-ass, any day. Actually his name was Jeff Totten, of the uppity Totten family, but that only made it worse. What nerve did he have, robbing the cradle, taking my daughter out in that fancy car? It was so frustrating. Jeff was eighteen and a freshman in the community college. Joy was only sixteen--going on seventeen as she liked to remind him--having skipped rapidly through school. She met Jeff while taking advanced college classes during her senior year in high school. Nate was certain the only reason Jeff wasn't going to an expensive private colleage was that his grades weren't good enough, or maybe he'd been caught doing drugs or drunk driving...or worse. No doubt it was something awful. One thing was certain, Jeff Totten was not good enough for his daughter. Nate caught himself grinding his teeth. *Gotta quit doing that before the dentist gets after me again.*

Nate looked around at the crowd. He began to pay close attention as the readers commenced introducing students whose names started with M. The name Sally Miller was never far from his mind. But, of course, Sally would be in her early twenties, now. *What am I thinking? This is crazy.* Nate silently kicked himself. He knew exactly how old Sally would be, and the date of her birthday. He shifted in his seat again and tried to surreptitiously adjust his trousers where they were binding. *Aw, hell, I guess I'll go down the steps and use the rest room.* The readers were only up to the P's. *Plenty of time before the grand finale.* Besides it would feel good to stretch his legs.

Nate stood up and started moving down the row, trying to avoid stepping on other people's feet or tripping on a wayward purse. "Excuse me, pardon me, please," he apologized as parents and family members of the graduates tried to get out of his way, bending their knees to one side or half-standing and scootching back in the narrow space.

One elderly gentleman took advantage of the opportunity to follow Nate. "I'm right behind you, buddy," he said in an overly loud tone. Obviously, the man was hard of hearing.

Nate smiled at him and nodded, "Come along" he gestured as they both chuckled.

"Shhh, quiet please," said one woman as Nate momentarily blocked her sight. She craned to one side. "That's my son!" she motioned frantically.

Nate quickly faded back, bumping into the elderly gentleman. "Oops, sorry."

The woman stood up and started to cheer, clap and wildly wave her arms.

Nate stood next to her and applauded politely, as well. What else could he do?

Nate had just celebrated his fifty-fourth birthday. Already he was noticing the "old-man's" affliction characterized by more frequent trips to the bathroom. This couldn't be happening, could it? "You're in the prime of your life," Nate's doctor assured him at his last checkup. Well, it was true, he still had his hair, most of it anyway. A little graying at the temples only made him look distinguished, his wife told him. Nate could still run a mile twice a week and had only let his belt out a few notches since he was a track star in high school.

Eventually Nate and his new pal made it down the three flights, across the marble-floored lobby and down another long flight to the basement rest rooms. They stood side by side at the urinals and made polite remarks.

"I suppose you are here for one of the grads," Nate offered.

"Yeah, actually there are two. Twins," he replied. "Grandkids," he added.

Nate nodded and mumbled, "Mmmm."

"And you?" asked the man as they both adjusted their underwear and zipped up.

"Daughter," said Nate, as they moved to wash their hands.

"You must be a proud papa."

"Oh yeah, proud, but worried, too."

"I get it," said the man sympathetically. "Kids, these days!"

"Yup, times have changed."

"Ya' think?' said the man, grinning as he pulled a couple paper towels out of the box on the wall and handed one to Nate. "You don't know the half of it."

"Oh she's a great kid. No problems there," said Nate, "It's that no-good boyfriend she's got." Nate had no idea why he was opening up to this gentleman.

"Ah, yes, I get it. I raised four daughters. Believe me, I didn't have a moment's peace until the last one was married off," he chuckled. "But, now I've got granddaughters. Seems like it never ends."

"Pity you, pal," said Nate.

"Problem is nobody bothers getting married, these days. It's awful."

"Oh no," said Nate. "I've yet to experience that."

"Oh yeah. Three of them are living in sin. All got good jobs. Why do they need husbands?"

"Living in sin?" Nate asked, unfamiliar with the term.

The man chuckled, "Never heard of living in sin, huh? Well, that's just an old-fashioned idea, I guess. Like me—out of date."

Nate sighed and held the door open, noticing for the first time how slow and stooped-over the old man seemed to be.

"Thank you, young man," said the fellow, "You go on back. I'm going to sit down here and watch the proceedings on television." He indicated a soft chair seated in front of a closed-circuit TV. "I'm not quite up to all those steps, twice in one day."

"I'd best get back," Nate responded as he turned to go.

"Good luck," called the man.

Something tells me I'm going to need it, Nate thought.

Ten minutes later Nate sagged back into his seat. Nan looked up and smiled, "Welcome back." Nate looked around at the empty seats. Nearly half the people had left already.

The last graduate ascended the stage as the reader stumbled over his name. *Who would name their kid Zachary Zane Zaremba? Good grief.*

After closing announcements. the new grads roared and threw their expensive hats into the air. *So much for that*, thought Nate. "Let's go," he said to Nan, as he stood to stretch.

~~~~~~

The three Goodriches joined the crowd outside as families strained their necks trying to find each other. It seemed that more than one group had agreed to meet beside the statue. This was one time when it helped to be six-foot-three-inches tall.

Nate's son, Rob, was even taller. At age nineteen and a junior at State university, Rob was home from college in time to attend his little sister's graduation. In three weeks' time he would be off again to Italy as part of an exchange program. But, for now, he was enjoying his visit at home and catching up with his old pals from high school. Truthfully, not many of them were still around, and so Rob had more time on his hands than he really wanted. Once you left home, things were never quite the same. Rob planned to crash the party where the newly minted graduates would be celebrating. While he checked out the fresh crop of eligible chicks, he would keep an eye on his little sister. Older and wiser, he knew what went on after those parties.

The hatless graduates moved back and forth, some carrying flowers and leather-bound diplomas, others with robes open, flying in the breeze. Nate's eyes roamed over the crowd as excited families reunited amid hugs and handshakes. His eyes were never still. It was part of his training, but also, without realizing it, he was always looking for a certain young woman in her early twenties--someone who looked like the Goodrich clan, but also resembled Nate's first wife, Ethel. Would he ever meet his lost daughter? Maybe someday, who knows? Nate snapped back to reality as Joy ran up and threw her arms around her mother, Nan, and then her dad and brother in a happy group hug.

~~~~~~

Nate knew he had to get some rest before he reported tomorrow on his assignment as a Federal Air Marshal. Over the years he had perfected the art of sleeping "with one ear open". He knew precisely when a car drew up in the driveway and parked with the lights off. Jeff and Joy would be out there doing God knows what. Twenty minutes later he heard the door click closed and stocking-clad feet creep up the stairs to her room. Nate's inner clock told him it was five o'clock without even opening an eye to check his watch. Next to him, Nan sighed and rolled over in her sleep. Apparently, Nan's motherly radar was tuned in, as well. Ten minutes later Rob's car returned. Heavier footsteps moved across the kitchen to the fridge, making no effort to be silent. Nate relaxed. His kids were home. He had one more hour to sleep before the bell rung for another work day.

Chapter 2 Sally

*A*cross the continent, Sally Millecan was already up and ready for work. She would report for duty serving on a cross-country flight for Alaska Airlines, an assignment for which she had waited weeks. Sally had worked hard to rise to a level in the company where she could pick and choose the plum assignments.

It had been her dream ever since she was a little girl playing with "Stewardess Barbie." Sally had applied for the job as a flight attendant right out of the two-year community college she attended.

Sally's single mom could not afford to send her to college and so Sally still had student loans to pay. That was okay. Her side job was paying off those loans. Sally loved her mother and appreciated the extra height with which Sally was endowed. It gave her an edge over other applicants for this good paying job.

Sometimes, in quiet moments, Sally wondered about that issue. Sally's mom was less than average height, and so there must have been some tall people back in Sally's lineage, somewhere. Could it have been from her father's side? Sally learned, at an early age, not to ask questions about her father. Her mother would shrug and put it off with a non-committal answer, insisting, "I never knew your father," or "I was never told."

Today, Sally would be a senior flight attendant on the mid-morning flight from the Washington D.C. Reagan International Airport to Sea-Tac, the Seattle-Tacoma International Airport in the US state of Washington, or (in the IATA code) DCA to SEA. This midday flight was very popular for big wigs such as politicians, Navy and Airforce Pentagon people, and employees of the major airplane manufacturer and defense contracting company located in the area, traveling between D.C. and Seattle.

This would be a long day. The flight would take more than seven hours altogether, with a stop in DFW, Dallas-Fort Worth International Airport, which was another busy hub for airplane employees and military contractors.

~~~~~~

Sally was working the first-class section. Dressed in her smart uniform, she greeted the passengers as they arrived.

"Good morning Sir," "Good morning Madam," "Welcome aboard," "May I take your coat?"

Sally had already served the crew with coffee, breakfast snacks, or their choice of a full breakfast. Now she turned toward the passengers and began to offer a variety of drinks and snacks. She was sensitive to each person's need to talk or not. A few words and a smile were enough for most people, ending with an offer to be of any assistance. But, for a nervous traveler, a longer conversation might be in order.

Sally loved working first-class. It allowed her the time and opportunity to give passengers personal service. She enjoyed meeting a variety of people, as different as snowflakes. She was a natural. It gave her the perfect opportunity to become acquainted with certain people, in particular the special people she needed to meet for her "part-time" job, on the side.

It wasn't anything dangerous, or illegal, so they said. She wasn't certain about that last part. Maybe it was a bit shady, but she didn't ask questions. She just snapped pictures, eavesdropped on conversations and reported, that was all.

Washington D.C. was overrun with lobbyists—influence peddlers, so to speak. It was just one big gravy-train. All Sally was doing is feeding at a little corner of the trough, perfectly legal, she was assured. Sally had no idea what became of her report, maybe nothing. Even though she was out of her comfort zone, it paid well, she reasoned. In ten months she would have her student loan paid off and then she would retire from this side job. After all, she could live quite well on her salary if she was careful, that is.

After a few weeks on this DCA-SEA run, Sally could spot the passengers who were involved with the aircraft compay, whether as buyers, suppliers or employees. She made it a point to memorize their names and greet them personally as they came on board. That would cause them to look up and smile. Occasionally, one of them would ask her out. She would thank them and point out that she wasn't allowed to fraternize with the guests. However, she might mention that she always stopped at the Starbucks on the airport mall after her trip, or one of the restaurants or bars. Invariably the gentleman or woman would meet her there. Sally would feign surprise. "Oh hello," she would say. "Weren't you just on the flight from D.C.?"

"Well, yes, as a matter of fact I was. May I join you?"

Sally would look around as if this was the only seat available. "It's a free country," she would say and gesture toward a seat across from her. After that it was a simple matter to inquire about the person's situation and circumstances. She had a way with people. After a drink or two it was easy for Sally to get the person to talk.

Sally never gave out her real name nor anything more than the simplest of honest details about herself. When pressed, oftentimes she made up a fantasy story, a different one each time. And she never allowed the man to pick up her check or touch anything personal. She made sure the waiter cleared away the dishes before they parted, lest the other person get her fingerprints off a glass. You never knew who was spying on whom. Not that it mattered, but Sally enjoyed spy novels, and had learned a thing or two. Sometimes she pretended it was a game and play-acted the role.

At the end of the day, alone in her room, she would write out her report by hand and put it in an envelope to mail the next day. The envelopes were already stamped and pre-addressed to a different post office box each time, in and around D.C. Sally was careful not to lick the envelopes, but her fingerprints were all over the paper. There was nothing she could do about that but try to wipe them away. It seemed a bit silly, but she was instructed the reports had to be done this way, to avoid having anything on her computer. The pictures were another matter. But Sally had been taught how to transfer them to a tiny memory chip and erase them from the special cell phone, provided. The memory card went into the envelope with her report, and every week or so she destroyed the phone and got another. Using the phone seemed somewhat conspicuous to Sally. But, she soon learned that people thought nothing of seeing a cell phone in someone's hand, even if it was pointed right at them.

The gentlemen and women targeted were airplane manufacturing company bigwigs and foreigners visiting the company headquarters. Rarely was it a politician, although they were persons of interest. Sally did not talk long with politicians, nor meet with them afterward. It was important to arouse no suspicion.

Sally had an uncanny ability to peg people right away. She made a private game of guessing their age, occupation and marital status as they entered the plane and took their seats. Later, as she met them she would try to find out how close she came. She usually guessed right more than half the time. Sometimes she had a perfect record. She could easily spot the bodyguards for the more important passengers. Some of them were so obvious! The one type that she had trouble spotting was the Federal Air Marshals. She knew they were on the flight somewhere, but they were so well trained in disguises that she was rarely successful in picking them out. It was a challenge for her, but mostly a process of elimination. If they weren't something else, then they must be Air Marshals. None would ever own up to it, and so how would she know? She wished she could tell, because she might need one someday.

~~~~~~

Another Work Day

The alarm clock vibrated at Nate's bedside. He had set the ringer on vibrate the night before. Even so, he shut it off immediately so as not to disturb Nan. She needed to rest after the busy day yesterday.

No such luxury was afforded Nate. Quietly he moved to the bathroom and shut the door before he turned on the light. He would take his shaving kit and toothbrush downstairs to the guest bathroom. No need to wake up the house, although he doubted that an earthquake would disturb the kids before noon. His bags were packed, his clothes had been set out the night before and coffee was waiting in the kitchen. Nate poured his first cup of coffee and went about getting ready for work. Only when he reported in for duty would he learn what city he would sleep in tonight. It could be any airline or any flight, a different one each time. He would be gone for three or four days before he saw his family again, traveling around the country, on first one flight and then another. The idea was to never be seen on the same flight twice, and never to become a familiar face to the flight crew and, most of all, the bad guys.

His height worked against him somewhat, but he compensated by wearing different clothes, hats, and sunglasses. They were not obvious disguises, but just non-descript and different from the outfit he wore yesterday. He had learned to vary his walk, the way he held his body, the timing of his speech, his accents and facial expressions.

The one thing he couldn't avoid was always carrying a case--a bag or backpack of some kind. In his checked luggage, he had a half-dozen different ones all of which were plain and simple on the outside but very special on the inside. His sophisticated communicator and weapons were well-hidden from view and available within a split-second's reach. They were manufactured from top secret high-tech components, impervious to airport security.

Nate traveled under any number of different names and identities. One of his problems was remembering who he was today. It helped that he always used the same first name, not his own, of course. He had to be friendly, but not too friendly with whomever his seatmate was at the time. Nate often took an aisle seat toward the back of the plane, so that he could observe everyone. But, even that was carefully scheduled, so that he wasn't always in the same place. Sometimes he sat in first-class. There could be others, like himself, on the same flight. Nate never knew for sure.

None of his friends, nor anyone in his family knew his actual occupation. They thought he was an airline pilot. Well, that wasn't so far off. He was licensed and could pilot almost any plane, in a pinch, if called upon. But, for the most part his job was not that glamourous. He liked to think of it as weeks of well-paid boring days, doing nothing except be prepared for a few seconds of abject terror.

~~~~~~

Paradise Valley

It was already past noon when the younger Goodrich sibling crawled out of bed, blinking at the bright light. Joy made her way into the bathroom for a quick nature call. Slipping into her favorite soft jeans and baggy sweatshirt, she padded barefoot into the kitchen.

"Hi Sis," said Rob, "How goes it?"

"Mmmm," grumbled Joy as she stumbled toward the coffeemaker.

"I'm afraid that's cold," said Rob. "Here, have a sip of mine while I warm yours up." He handed his cup to Joy and turned to get a fresh one out of the cupboard. Filling it to within a half inch of the rim, he set it in the microwave and hit the thirty second button twice.

Joy stared, set the cup down, and shoved the hair out of her face.

"Sit down," offered Rob as he pulled out a seat.

23

Joy sank onto the stool and leaned her chin on her hands, elbows on the counter.

A minute later Rob placed the cup of coffee in front of her along with a spoon, a bowl and box of cold cereal. He took his place across from her and silently shoved the sugar bowl and carton of milk across the kitchen island toward her.

Joy automatically added sugar and milk to her coffee and stared at nothing. She took a sip, testing the coffee, and then continued slouching on one elbow while drinking.

Rob opted to wait for her to come online for the day.

After a few minutes, Joy straightened up, reached for the cereal and filled her bowl half way. She added milk and sugar and began to eat. Slowly life was returning.

Meanwhile Rob refilled his coffee and made toast.

"Toast?" he asked, as he placed a small plate of toast onto the island counter.

"Thanks," said Joy, swallowing the last bite of cereal.

Rob removed her spoon and empty bowl to the dishwasher, opened the cupboard for peanut butter and the fridge for strawberry jam. "Here," he said, as he placed a butter dish and a knife along with the other items.

Joy managed a half smile as she began to slather her toast and take the first bite. "Help yourself," she said.

"No thanks, I'm good," said Rob. He leaned back and took her measure. "Congratulations on your honors," he offered.

She nodded, "Thanks."

"I always knew you were the smartest one," he smiled.

"Not true," she shook her head, "not true at all."

"What do you mean, not true?"

"Being book smart doesn't count when it comes to life, does it?"

"Huh?"

She leaned on her hand, again, sighed and looked defeated.

"What do you mean, life?" Rob prodded.

"Men!" she exclaimed, as if he should know.

"Oh that," Rob stifled a chuckle. "I have the same problem with women."

"Oh, you do not," she countered. "Women just fall all over you. You have your pick."

"I beg to differ," he denied, weakly.

"Ha!" she huffed and swatted at the hair in her face.

Rob eyed her closely and reached for the toast and butter. "I guess I'm still hungry." He leaned back and took a bite. "So, tell me," he said, "what brought this on?"

Joy shrugged and sniffed, "I was so stupid."

"I doubt that."

"Yeah, I was," she insisted.

"So, what happened with Mr. Big Wheel College Man?"

"That's just it. You've got it exactly right."

"Mm," Rob nodded and worked on his toast. "Left you high and dry, I take it."

"Not funny!"

"Then what?"

"Well, maybe he is the one left high and dry."

"I see," said Rob.

"Do you?"

"Well, I can guess."

"Go ahead, you tell me."

"Okay, if that is what you want," Rob had to make sure.

"Yeah," she said, looking straight at him fighting to keep the tears from escaping.

"Well, okay, I'm guessing that Mr. College Man thought he should receive special favors in return for spending his good money on taking you out."

She nodded.

"And so, depending on what kind of a man he is, maybe he wouldn't take no for an answer."

She sniffed and wiped at her eyes.

"And so, you, being a nice girl, tried to be polite."

She nodded.

"And he, being stronger, became too aggressive."

She looked up at Rob in silence, feeling chagrined.

Rob reached for a box of tissues and handed them to her. "How did you get out of it, Joy?"

She looked away.

"Did you shove him, hit him?"

Joy nodded, took a tissue and blew her nose.

"Did you get away?" Rob asked, fearing the answer.

"Yes, I got away. He started calling me awful names. I opened the door and ran into the house," she sobbed out and started crying in earnest. "Awful names!"

Rob reached for her hand. "Honey, you did absolutely the right thing. And you are none of those names. He is a jerk."

"Really?"

"Really, as true, as true as the world is old. You did just right, and he knew exactly what he was doing." Rob waited. "Do you want me to go beat him up?"

"What?" she exclaimed.

"That's what big brothers do, hon. That's my job." He waited.

"I guess you don't need to do that," she answered. "He's probably through with me."

Rob laughed. "I think you are a whole lot smarter about men than you thought. You're right. He won't be around again. He'll move on to greener pastures. There are lots better men out there. Men who will treat you with respect. Just wait."

Joy managed a half-smile.

"There is only one reservation about this. That is, if he should start spreading lies about you, I want you to tell me. I'll fix his wagon."

"Thanks, Rob."

"You're welcome. There will be more and better men in your life. Don't worry. Just remember, I'm here. Anytime you need me to check out a guy, just call. Okay?"

"Okay," she said with a big smile. "I'll remember that." She rose and started clearing the dishes away. "But, what do I do if you're not around?"

"Well, first of all I still have pals here in Paradise Valley. Just send me an SOS. But, second, and I know you don't believe this now, but you have a father who will understand and will protect you with his life. Not all girls can say that."

"Oh, I'd die if Daddy knew."

"Probably you would be embarrassed, but someday you may need him. Hang in there, hon. We are both here to protect you. And don't overlook your wise mom, when you need advice."

"You've got to be kidding."

"Not at all. Moms have a sixth sense about these things. They can spot a phony around their daughter in seconds."

Just then, Nan walked into the kitchen. "Hi kids," she said.

"Hi, Mother."

"Did you get something to eat?"

"Yes, we're good," Rob answered. "I've put my cooking skills to work."

Nan smiled, "Toast and cold cereal, I see."

Rob clutched his heart, "You wound me."

"Not at all," said Nan. "I'll be glad to let you cook dinner, if you want. Looks as if it is too late for lunch."

"Okay, you're on," said Rob. "I learned how to cook at my mother's knee. Let's see, where's the number for Pizza Hut?"

Nan laughed and turned to Joy, "Did you have a good time at the party, hon?"

"Great time, Mom."

"That's good, honey. These are memories you will always cherish."

Joy and Rob gave each other meaningful looks.

"That bad, huh?" said Nan.

"I told you so," muttered Rob to Joy, under his breath. They both laughed.

"What's so funny?" asked Nan.

Joy looked at Rob for help.

"Inside joke, Mom," said Rob. "You're the best."

"Thanks, Rob, I think," she retorted. "So, what are your plans this afternoon?"

"Um, well …" Joy shrugged.

"I'm meeting some of the fellas," said Rob. "You want to go along?" he asked looking at Joy.

"Well, I guess so. Depends on what you are doing."

"Nothing great. But, we plan to meet at the rec center and hang out, maybe do a little bowling, play some pool, be back here in time to watch the ball game, get supper for the three of us and anyone else who wants to come along."

"Isn't Daddy home?" Joy looked at Nan.

"No, honey, he had to go to work early this morning."

"Oh," Joy's voice fell. "Well then, sure, Rob, thanks for dragging your little sister along."

"Oh baby, you don't know how much those guys have begged me to bring you."

"Sure, right, and pigs fly, too."

They all laughed.

Rob chucked Joy under the chin and smiled. "Be ready at 1:15, Okay?" He turned to leave the room.

"I'll be ready, and thanks," said Joy to his retreating back, thinking how Rob had changed since he left home. It was like the frog had turned into a prince.

Chapter 3 Nate

A Typical Evening on the Job

*T*he Yellow cab pulled up in front of the Airport Marriott. Nate waited while the driver popped open the trunk and hurried around to open his door. Carefully glancing around, Nate saw nothing unusual. Dressed in soft slacks, a knit golf shirt and jacket with comfortable sneakers on his feet, Nate alighted from the cab, an aging cloth briefcase in his left hand, his carry-on bag in his right. Setting the smaller bag atop the other, he steadied it with one hand while he reached into his pocket and pulled out a bill— one that he has previously selected from his wallet. Nate knew the exact cost of this cab ride, plus a twenty percent tip, rounded up to the nearest dollar. He had learned not to fumble with a wallet when exposed, out in the open like this. It was a small detail, but his safety depended on attention to a lot of little things.

"Thank you, sir," said the cabbie as he pocketed the bill and walked back to the driver's side.

Meanwhile, the hotel doorman had lifted Nate's one larger bag from the trunk of the cab. "Welcome to the Marriott, sir," said the doorman. "Checking in?"

"Yes," said Nate as he grabbed the handle on his carry-on bag keeping it close and making sure that his body protected the bag. He could never let anyone else touch this special suitcase. "I'll take this one, and you can bring that other bag up later. Just leave it in the room." He handed the doorman a tip.

Less than a minute later, Nate pulled out the long handle of his bag, and wheeled it up to the counter. He had been in this city before, but never this hotel. While he was fond of the

Marriott chain, he could never stay in the same hotel twice. If possible, he stayed in a different hotel each time, sometimes near and sometimes farther away from the airport. All this silliness might seem right out of a spy novel, but if he was ever discovered or "unmasked" by America's enemies, he would be disqualified for this job. Anonymity was essential. Since 9/11, no terrorist had succeeded in taking down an American airliner thanks to the diligence and expertise of this hidden army of which Nate was a part.

Nate placed his cloth bag on the counter, and kept his left hand on the other bag. He pushed one of several credit cards toward the clerk. He carried four sets of identity for this four-day trip.

"Welcome to the Marriott," she said as she picked up his credit card and glanced at the name. "Do you have a reservation, Mr. Galloway?"

Nate shook his head no. Nate did not always make reservations. Sometimes he would make a reservation and cancel it, and sometimes he would stay at a different hotel without canceling the first one.

"Did you have a pleasant trip, Mr. Galloway?" she asked as she turned to her computer and deftly typed in his name.

"Yes, thank you," said Nate.

The woman's fingers flew across the keyboard. She swiped his card and tendered it back with a smile. Handing him a pen, she said, "If you will just sign right here, we'll have you in your room right away."

Nate scribbled something on the dotted line, picked up the envelope containing the key-card to his room, glanced at the room number and put the key into his pocket.

"Do you need help with your bags?"

Nate shook his head, "No thank you, I'm good."

"Take the A elevators, sir," she said, pointing left, "down this way. If there is anything else you need, feel free to call. Enjoy your stay at the Marriott," she smiled again.

Nate pocketed his credit card, picked up his cloth briefcase and turned toward the elevators, pulling his bag.

He would wait for an empty elevator before entering it.

Nate would repeat this procedure four more times, in four different ways, using four different names, in four cities across the United States, before he made it back home. It was just another job to him for which he was well trained. Looking forward to retirement in maybe ten years, he doubted he would ever want to fly again, certainly not in a coach seat, and never, ever in the center coach seat. Well, he had only gotten stuck in the center seat once and that was a mistake. In his job, he had to be on the aisle so he could get out at a moment's notice.

Had he ever taken down any bad guys? Yes, more than once. But, so far, he had managed to keep it entirely quiet, or to get away before anyone from the media took his picture or discovered his identity. Even if they did, he would probably be able to discard that identity and vanish, so long as they didn't discover his real name. Most arrests happened so smoothly, the passengers were not aware of what had happened and that was exactly the way Nate liked it.

~~~~~~

A Fun Afternoon

Rob and Joy said goodbye to Mom and left in his car to pick up his pals for their afternoon of fun at the recreation center. Rob pulled up to the curb, put the transmission into "park" and prepared to go up to their friend's house and ring the bell.

Before he could go far, the two young men came around the side, all ready to go. Apparently, they had been watching and left the house by the back door.

"Hi Guys," said Rob. "Come on and join the party. Tom and Elvin, I'd like you to meet my sister Joy. Say hi to Joy."

Joy rolled down the window to greet the men. "Hi," she said with little enthusiasm.

"Hello, darlin'," said Elvin as he opened her door and started to get in beside her.

"Whoa, wait just one minute there," said Tom. "I think Joy might rather sit next to me."

"Me first," said Elvin in mock horror.

"You expect me to sit back here all alone?" Tom whined, playing it to the hilt.

Rob was enjoying this immensely. He had tipped off the guys to make a play for Joy, saying her ego needed a boost.

Tom took Elvin's arm and tried to gently pull him back. "No, me first," said Tom.

"Let's let the lady choose," said Elvin.

They both grinned at her and assumed their best poses.

"All right," said Tom. "You would rather sit next to me, wouldn't you, Joy?" He gave her a devastating smile and ran a hand over his hair.

"Uh," said Joy, looking at Rob for help. He just laughed. "You both seem like such nice young men," she said, turning back toward the two, with a brighter smile. "Why don't we three all sit in the back. I'll sit in the middle."

"But, that's too uncomfortable for a nice lady like you," said Elvin. "You sit by the window, and I'll sit in the middle."

"Oh no you don't," said Tom.

"Boys, boys, let's get going. Joy, you stay right here beside me, and both you men, get in the back seat," said Rob with the voice of authority. "I don't trust either one of you."

The disgruntled men got in back, but both leaned forward and tried to engage Joy in conversation.

"Seat belts," commanded Rob. "It's only a ten-minute drive. Control yourselves!" He laughed.

The rest of the day, the two men vied for her attention. At the pool table they insisted on helping her with her technique. At the air hockey game they argued over who would be her partner. At table tennis, they eagerly chased after the ball when it flew away and then deliberately let her win. And now, they fought over who would pull out her chair, finally agreeing to share the task, one on each side.

Seated around a small table with snacks and drinks, Rob reached for the check. Joy had left for a few minutes to visit the rest room. "I'll get this," he said. "It's the least I can do to pay you back. You did a great job of picking up her spirits. Thanks."

"No problem," said Elvin. "She's a lovely person."

"It was fun watching her perk up," said Tom. "I hope we didn't lay it on too thick."

"Well, anyway, I think we got that Jeff Totten off her mind and out of her life," said Rob.

"Jeff Totten, you say?" asked Tom.

"Yeah, Jeff Totten. Why do you ask?"

Tom motioned with his head, "Over there."

"That's him?" asked Rob.

"You didn't know?"

"I guess not." Rob gazed at Totten. "So that's the s.o.b."

"Do either of you know his full initials?" asked Elvin.

"All I know is J.T.," answered Rob.

"It's J.E.T. for Jeff Earnest Totten," said Tom. "I knew him in high school. What a jerk! Why do you ask?"

"I don't think you will like the words written on the wall in the men's john," warned Elvin.

"What words?" asked Rob.

"Um ... something about a girl named Joy and signed J.E.T."

Rob blanched. "I've got to see this," he launched out of his seat, almost knocking over the chair.

"Stall number six," called Elvin.

"What's he going to do?" Tom wondered. The two of them watched as Rob disappeared into the men's room.

Elvin looked at Tom and shrugged. "I wouldn't want to be J.E.T. right now."

A minute later Rob emerged, stalked directly to Jeff Totten's table and towered over him, menacingly. "Stand up, you coward."

"Who the hell are you, ass-hole?" asked Jeff.

"Mr. Goodrich to you," said Rob through clenched teeth as he took a firm hold of Jeff's shirt and lifted him from his chair.

"Take your hands off me," Jeff tried to push him away, as the other men at the table watched in surprise.

"You're coming with me," said Rob as he all-but-dragged Totten to the men's room and stall number six. Pointing to the offending words and the signature J.E.T., he demanded, "Is this your rotten-ass work?"

Totten paled and said nothing.

"Is this your work?" Rob shoved him against the wall, doubling up his fist in Totten's face.

Totten giggled nervously. "So what if it is?"

"I don't take kindly to lies about my sister, jackass!"

"Your sister had a really sweet ass," Totten simpered.

Rob's fist connected with the man's face as his knee took him in the groin. "Take it back," he growled.

Totten groaned and doubled over in pain.

"What did you say?"

"Your sister is very nice," Jeff hissed, "I was just kidding."

"What?"

"Joy Goodrich is still a virgin."

"That's better," said Rob. "Try harder."

"I never touched her," he gasped.

"Louder!"

"I'm a jackass!"

"That's exactly right. Now, I want those lies removed from this wall, and any other place you may have put them. And I want you to take back any more shit you have spread around. If I hear so much as a hint of it, you will be extremely sorry, do you hear? You've been warned, asshole." Rob let go with his hands.

Totten slid to the floor, holding his crotch.

Back at the table, Rob released his fists, took a deep breath and sighed. "I think it's time to leave this place," he said.

"What did you do?"

Rob eyed the group of five tough guys seated around the Totten table. "We may be a bit outnumbered," he spoke wryly.

Joy walked up, just as everyone stood. They smiled at her as if nothing had happened. Rob glanced at his watch. "Are you ready to go home, babe?"

"Okay, if you want to. Whatever you say," said Joy. "I had a wonderful time. Thank you all, very much." She smiled at each one, in turn.

"Let me help you with your jacket," offered Tom.

"Let me take your arm," said Elvin.

The four of them walked past Totten's table without a backward glance.

~~~~~~

Room Service

Nate ordered dinner from room service and settled down in his hotel room for the evening. He would call home later. But, first he would check his email and do a bit of research online. Idly, he typed in the name Sally Miller just to see if anyone new would pop up. He had done this so many times before, he didn't expect anything. There were the usual people. Sally Miller was such a common name. How easy it was to get lost reading some of the cockamamie stories!

There was the former slave who claimed she immigrated from Germany and should have been free. Nate wasn't sure what that was about.

Sally Miller, the artist, invited people to check out her online studio, as did Sally Miller, the designer of dresses.

An intriguing Sally Miller was interviewed online about her tell-all book boasting that she was mistress to a former president. Could this be the same one as Sally Miller the porn star? Nate chuckled.

He had to be careful that he didn't wander too far down that path and get his computer infected.

Of course, his first baby's name could have been changed by now, and she could be anywhere, or nowhere. Nate shuddered to think of the possibility she could even be dead. One thing was for sure, Sally Miller's mother had successfully vanished without a trace and had taken the baby with her. For an intensive time after it happened, Nate had exhausted his resources looking for them, until, eventually he had met Nan and fallen in love. It was only then that he was able to let go of the past and begin to move on with his life today.

It all happened a long time ago. Nevertheless, knowing that Sally's 21st birthday was this month, had brought it to mind. But there was no use dwelling on it. Perhaps, someday fate would bring them together again. Life sure had its twists and turns.

Nate sighed and closed his computer. He would call Nan and then settle down to watch TV until he fell asleep.

No sooner had Nate relaxed on the bed and picked up his phone than it vibrated in his hand. He looked at the caller ID and smiled. "Hello, sweetheart. I was just about to call you."

"Hi darling. Isn't it uncanny? I always know when you are calling." She chuckled. "How was your flight?" Nan asked.

"Nice flight, honey. No weather delays and we arrived ten minutes early."

"Good work, darling. You weren't speeding on the tarmac, were you?" she joked.

"Tailwinds, dearest. So, what's new with you? Anything?"

"The kids cooked supper for us. Wasn't that sweet?"

"Well, finally! It's about time our investment started to pay off," Nate answered. "What did you have?"

"Would you believe pizza?"

"That hardly counts as cooking, does it?"

She laughed, "Agreed. But, Rob insisted that counted because he had to put it in the oven and watch it."

"Oh, one of those ready-to-bake pizzas, huh?"

"Yes, I think so. They certainly didn't make it from scratch."

Nate laughed, "Like father, like son."

"No comment," said Nan. "Oh, by the way, your former sister-law called. They are moving."

"Oh really? Did Major Eastman get transferred or something?"

"Yes, guess what—they are moving to Dayton."

"Dayton, Ohio?"

"Yes. You know there is a large Airforce base there."

"Well, that's good. I'm happy he didn't get deployed overseas."

"Yeah, me too. They want us to come for Thanksgiving."

"So soon?" asked Nate starting to worry already. Thanksgiving was one of the busiest travel periods of the year. It would be all-hands-on deck for the Air Marshall service.

"I guess Cynthia and Sky plan to buy a house right away."

"Must be the Major thinks this will be a permanent post for him."

"She didn't say, and I didn't ask, of course."

"Well, do you want to go? For Thanksgiving, I mean."

"Don't you?" she asked.

"Not really. I'd rather stay home with you and our own kids."

"Me too. I'll go ahead and send our regrets."

"Thanks, Nan. That will be nice of you. I know you have a way with words."

"You're welcome, I think." She chuckled. It was easy to let herself get bamboozled by Nate. She loved him more than life.

"Well, I've got an early wakeup call," said Nate.

"Yes, dear, you need your beauty sleep. Thanks for the call, darling," she laughed.

"No, you called me, remember?"

"Oh yeah. Well, thanks for your time." She laughed again.

"You're welcome, my sweet. For you--anytime."

"Bye-by. Love you."

"Bye-bye you sweet thing. Miss you already. Love you back."

Nate and Nan never ended a call without saying love you. Life was too fragile. Nate clicked off, leaned back and picked up the remote. He smiled, thinking how lucky he was. He'd probably have to work a run or two the day before Thanksgiving and maybe after as well, but there was a good likelihood he would have the actual Thanksgiving Day off, if he could get back home on time, that is.

Nate took some papers out of his briefcase and settled back on the pillows to do a bit of studying. He would study the names, faces and dossier on the latest persons of interest that the FBI was following. Nate would familiarize himself with the facts and memorize the faces and descriptions of as many as possible before turning himself in for the night. This helped to allow those faces to sink into his memory bank while he slept. He was always scanning the crowds for faces, sharpening his ability to recall hundreds of bad guys.

Chapter 4 Sally's Mother

*S*ally Millecan had a one-day layover in Seattle, from her flight attendant's job with Alaska Airlines— enough time to slip over the border to see her mom. It was not a pleasant duty but one she accepted. As the only child, it fell to her to look after her mom as much as possible. This was another reason that she hung onto this Sea-Tac assignment. Otherwise she might have to take vacation days to go to Vancouver. Not a good idea.

The elder-care nursing home was in a small rural community twenty miles outside of Vancouver. Getting there involved somewhat of a hassle, but Sally had flown there enough times to make it routine. It was one o'clock before she pulled into the parking lot in her rental car. It had been a nice day to drive along the coast. Taking the coastal highway was out of her way, but she had the time today, and so she permitted herself the indulgence of driving one of the world's most spectacular scenic highways.

Sally stopped at the desk to check in. "I'm here to see my mother, Ferrell Millecan."

The woman checked the name on her computer. "Yes, she's in 301B. Lunch time is over and so she should be in her room. Shall I get someone to take you up?"

"No thank you, I can find it," Sally braced herself for the walk down the hall. This was the nicest elder-care home she could find for mom, but still the sounds, odors and the old people made her uncomfortably aware of how short and fragile life is. Because of her mother's condition, she had to be in a nursing home that took care of the least capable ones, those with mental deterioration, like her mom, and those with end-of-life illnesses needing total nursing care. The doors were open allowing those patients to be heard who were babbling incoherently, moaning or crying out. Some folks were in the hallways shuffling along with their walkers while others were slumped in wheelchairs seemingly asleep or just unaware of their surroundings.

Sally found her mom strapped into a wheelchair parked with her back to the window, staring blankly at a baseball game blaring on the TV. Sally reached for the remote and put it on mute. Her mother's suite-mate could now be heard snoring loudly in the other bed.

Sally touched her mother's arm to get her attention. Ferrell looked up and made a noise low in her throat.

"Hello Mother," said Sally. "I'm here to see you today."

The woman looked at her, seemingly unable to understand. "What?" she almost shouted.

Sally realized that Ferrell's hearing aids were not in place. She walked over to the bedside table and pulled open a drawer. The case was right there where it always was. Sally opened the case and took out two hearing aids. Testing one, she realized the battery was dead. She sorted through the drawer for replacement batteries. Finding two, she inserted them into the proper compartments and tossed out the old batteries. "Here, Mom, put these on," she said, handing them to her mother, one at a time.

Ferrell remembered what they were, and so she put one in her ear. "I hate these things," she grumbled. "Makes my ears hurt. Damn batteries keep going dead. Cost too much."

"It's okay, Mom. You can take them out later. Put the other one in so we can have a little chat."

"Chat?" asked Ferrell as she fumbled with the aid and dropped it on the floor. This was the third set of aids Sally had bought this year. Something always happened to them. Either Ferrell wore them in the shower, or she lost them, or she dropped one on the floor and ran over it with her wheelchair.

Sally sighed, picked up the aid from the floor and wiped it with a tissue. "Here Mom, let's try again." This time Sally kept her hands close, in case the aid dropped. Ferrell got the aid installed and gazed at Sally.

"Hello, Mother," Sally smiled and tried once more.

"Who are you?" Ferrell asked in a quieter voice.

"I'm Sally, your daughter, remember me?"

"I have a daughter?"

"Yes, you do."

"How come you never come see me?"

"I come to see you a lot, Mother. I was here just last month for your birthday, remember?"

"My birthday? When was that?"

"Last month, Mother."

"No, I don't have birthdays, no more birthdays." Ferrell shook her head and pointed to the ball game. "That's my team you know," she crowed like a little girl.

"Yes, they are good, aren't they? What do you say I push you down the hall to the sun room where we can talk? Would you like that, Mother?"

"You know where it is?"

"Yes, I do. The sun room is nice, and quiet. We can talk."

"Okay, if you're sure. I've never been there."

"Yes, you have, Mother, you've just forgotten."

"Oh. I wish I could remember things," sighed Ferrell.

Sally took hold of the wheelchair and pushed her mother down the hall to a visitor's area, hoping it would be quiet. They were in luck. No one else was around. Sally pushed her mother into a pleasant spot and pulled up a chair. Sitting next to her mother, Sally took the woman's hand.

"Who are you?" asked Ferrell.

"I'm Sally, your daughter—Sally Millecan."

Ferrell squinted at her. "That's a lie, you're not my daughter."

"Yes, Mother, I'm your daughter, Sally Millecan," she said patiently. She expected this kind of thing and took no offense. There could be times when Ferrell had periods of lucidity and other times when she was lost. Sally lived and hoped for those few lucid times.

"You're not my daughter. I know my own daughter. Her name is Sally Miller," Ferrell insisted.

This fantasy happened sometimes. Sally just took it in stride. She laughed, "Oh yes, Mother. How could I forget? My name is Sally Miller, just as you said." She squeezed her mother's hands in hers.

Ferrell nodded in satisfaction and joined in the laughter. "I guess I ought to know my own daughter's name, don't you think?"

"Would you like to play some cards, Mother? Or can I read to you?"

"No thank you. I guess I'll go back and watch the ball game, now."

"Sure, Mother. I'll take you back."

"Thank you. I'm a little tired."

Ferrell was asleep by the time they reached 301B. Sally positioned her in front of the TV, turned the ball game on mute and lovingly tucked the lap-robe around her mother. Should she remove the hearing aids? Maybe not this time, but she would leave a note at the desk.

Driving back to the airport, she replayed the visit in her mind, pondering why her mother insisted her name was Miller, not Millecan. Probably a name from some soap opera her mother saw. There was no explanation for these things, but it nagged her. Sally wished she had had time to bring up the subject of her 21st birthday. Maybe it would have prodded her mother's old memories. So many things were lost in time, details about her birth and childhood that only Ferrell could tell her, if only she could remember.

These visits never seemed to take as long as planned. Sally's flight back to Seattle didn't leave until five o'clock. There was time to drive by the house where she spent some time growing up, in one of the Vancouver neighborhoods. They had moved around several times. Sally wasn't even sure of all the places they had lived. She had so many questions.

She had to circle around several times before she found the place. A lot had changed. The houses were almost alike, but she remembered it as one of her favorite times. At least it wasn't a tiny apartment in a crowded high-rise tenement, like some of the places they had lived. Those all ran together. This house was better. It had a yard with a tree she could climb, a back porch and a swing. She had her own room with a window looking out over the back yard. Also, she loved the school, only three blocks away. She could walk to school with friends, such as she had. Should she go up and knock on the door? No, there wasn't a good reason to do that. What would people think? It was not a fabulous house, anyway, just a special memory to her.

They never stayed in one place long enough to keep friends. Sally never knew any aunts or uncles, or grandparents. Her mom said they were dead and Sally accepted that, but it was lonely for her mother. Not that Sally lacked for friends. She made friends almost as quickly as she forgot them when they moved on.

Would there be anyone who remembered her? Any teachers? She felt almost like a person without a past. But, that wasn't true. It was out there somewhere. There was just so much she would never know or understand. For instance, why did they always live in Canada when Sally was born an American? Was her mother a citizen? Someday she would have to find out, but where to start looking?

Surely the nursing home would know. Maybe she could go online and find something. Sally made up her mind to do some digging—for what she wasn't sure.

Paradise Valley-Officer McGillicuddy

A couple of days had passed since Nan and Nate Goodrich's son, Rob, had the confrontation with the Totten kid. Nothing more had happened and so Rob felt relieved. So far, he hadn't heard from Totten's lawyer on an accusation of assault. Thank goodness, no cop had come knocking on the door. Rob's dad would not be pleased if that happened.

Rob was busy getting ready to fly to Italy, his other friends were occupied with their lives and girl-friends, and so Rob put it out of his mind until some odd things started to happen. It wasn't anything you could put your finger on. Maybe his cell phone would ring and no one would be there, or strange lights would shine in his bedroom at night.

With a list of things to pick up at the mall, Rob left the house by the front door. Keys in hand, he glanced at his car parked outside in the driveway. Oh my God! What on earth? Rob took off on a run. Something was spattered all over his car. Rob reached out a finger to touch it and then he backed off. The odor was horrific. All over the ground were broken egg shells. Someone had rotten-egged his car. Oh no! Rob gasped and looked around for help. No one was nearby. And then he saw the house. His heart sank. Eggs were running down the bricks. He ran his hand through his hair, then slumped his shoulders, sighed and shook his head when the realization hit. This was vandalism, requiring more professional cleanup than Rob could do on his own. He had to get help.

Slowly Rob moved away from the disaster and sank down to sit on the porch step. His mind went over the alternatives. What should he do? He hated it, but there was only one right thing to do. Rob sighed, drew out his cell phone and dialed 911.

"You have dialed 911. If this is an emergency press 1, if not, press 2."

Rob pressed 2.

"What is the nature of your problem? Please press 1 for police, 2 for fire, 3 for illness or injury, 4 to return to the main menu for emergency."

Rob pressed 1.

"Paradise Valley police department. How may I direct your call?"

Rob was happy to hear a real person.

"I need to report vandalism to my home and car, please."

"One moment, sir, and I will connect you with a duty officer."

"Sergeant Draff, how may I help you?"

"Hello?" said Rob.

"Hello, go ahead, please."

"Hello Sergeant. This is Robert Goodrich, 2010 Willow Avenue. I just discovered that someone has rotten-egged my car and the bricks on my parents' house."

"Rotten-egged your car and house—is that correct?" asked Sergeant Draff, smiling to himself.

"Yessir."

"Is it something you can clean up yourself?"

"No, it is extensive, Sergeant. Not just one egg--dozens. The car is covered, and the house ... well I haven't looked closely, but I know it will require professional people to clean it up."

"Is there any further damage?"

"I don't know. I just discovered it and called you right away."

"All right, sir, I have your report."

"Is that all you can do?"

"Do you wish to file a complaint?"

"I might," said Rob thinking of Jeff Totten.

"I have a patrol car on the way. Can you wait right there?"

"Yes, I'll wait. How long will it be?"

"Just a few minutes. Don't leave."

"Thank you."

"Anything else I can help you with?"

"That's all. Thank you."

"Goodbye, then."

"Goodbye."

Rob hung up, thinking *What should I do?* Geez, he hated to call Mom. He took a deep breath and blew it out through his lips. Gotta do it. I'll call the house phone first. Rob dialed the number and waited while it rang four times.

"Hello?" Nan sounded breathless.

"Mom, it's me. Sorry to bother you."

"What? Honey, you're no bother. Is something wrong?" She knew he had left to go shopping.

"Well no, I mean yes, a little."

"What happened Rob?"

"Well, I found some damage to my car, and so I had to call it in. Didn't want you to be surprised."

"What damage? Call what in? Call who? Where are you?"

"I'm right here, Mom, on the front porch."

Nan hung up the phone without saying goodbye. She dashed for the front door, threw it open and stepped outside.

Rob stood.

Nan gasped. She came to a halt beside Rob. "What happened? What is that junk all over your car? Is that paint?" She started forward down the sidewalk.

Rob stopped her. "Mother, please, stay back." He took her arm, and gently tried to pull her back.

Nan turned toward him. That's when she saw the house. Both hands flew to her mouth as she gasped, "Awwoh!" She turned toward Rob with tears starting to form.

"It'll clean up, Mom," said Rob.

"B-but," she shook her head, "What? Why?"

"Someone threw eggs on it, Mom … on the house and on my car."

Nan turned to look more closely at the damage.

"Don't go up there, Mom."

"Why not?"

"We need to wait for the patrol car."

"What patrol car?"

"I called the police,"

"You did?"

"Yeah, I had to report it, Mom, for the insurance company."

"Oh." Nan crossed her arms and started to rub her bare skin.

Rob put one arm around her. "You're shivering, Mom. Why don't you go inside? I'll wait for the patrol car."

Nan paused for a moment. "You're right, Rob. I am a little chilly. I'll get a sweater," she said and turned toward the door.

Rob tried to dissuade her. "Mom, you don't need to wait with me. I'm okay. It's just a simple vandalism report. You go on with your work or whatever you were doing. I'll take care of this."

Nan hesitated.

"Go on in, Mom. I'll be fine." Rob wasn't eager for her to overhear his conversation with the cop.

Nan took another look at the damage, slowly turned and went back inside. Rob could see her peeking out the window and hoped she would leave. Maybe if he sat down, she'd get bored. Rob returned to the steps, plunked down and rested his head on his hands.

It was another ten minutes, or so, before the marked police car arrived. Another couple of minutes passed while the officer spoke to dispatch and appeared to be writing on something. At last a uniformed policewoman emerged from the vehicle and walked around Rob's car, snapping pictures. Rob stood quietly, waited and watched while she took more pictures of the house. He couldn't help but notice her long blond braid hanging below her officer's cap and her neat round bottom encased by a smart dark-blue uniform. A gun was holstered on her right side, and a communicator was attached to one shoulder. She spoke quietly as she walked around. Rob realized that she wasn't talking to herself. She was either reporting her observations or merely recording them. He could imagine what she was saying as she looked the house and neighborhood over and then turned toward him and spoke a few sentences while gazing directly at him. Finally she stepped forward.

"You reported an incident of vandalism," she stated.

"Yes, officer, I called in a while ago," he glanced at his watch and added, "About twenty minutes, I guess."

"And your name is ...?"

"Robert Goodrich."

"Age?"

"Nineteen."

"Address. Occupation?"

"This is my home," Rob stated, wondering why there were so many questions, "but I am attending State University."

"Student," she said as she wrote. "Why are you home?"

"This is summer break. I'll be here for a few more days until I leave for a term in Italy." What would it take to break this woman's professional demeanor?

"Thank you for coming." Rob smiled as broadly as he could, considering what was happening.

She looked up from what she was writing. "It's my job," she stated without cracking a smile. "And now, you reported this as vandalism. What led you to make that statement?"

"Well, no one in the family would do this."

"Is that so?" she said as if she doubted it. "No arguments, no one in the family was upset about something?" She wrote rapidly.

"Of course not. What are you inferring?"

She merely gazed directly at him. "We make no judgements. I'm here to investigate a complaint."

"Of course," said Rob, "and doing a great job, I might add." She stopped.

"And your name is?" asked Rob.

"McGillicuddy. Officer McGillicuddy."

"Thank you, Officer McGillicuddy. Very nice name."

She chose to ignore Rob's attempt to flirt. She had seen it all. "And now, Mr. Goodrich," she said, with the emphasis on Mr., "do you have any idea why someone would do this?"

"No," Rob answered, choosing to keep his opinion to himself. Wasn't it obvious?

"A neighbor, maybe? Does anyone have a grudge?"

"On my folks? No, of course not."

"This is your car, isn't it?"

"Yes."

"Not your parents' car?"

"It's my car, in my name. I use it at school. But, as I said, I'm home for a couple of weeks."

"Well then, who has a grudge against you?"

How did she know? Rob looked away. She waited for his answer, as seconds mounted. A full minute passed. Rob started to sweat.

"Who did this?" she prodded.

"Well ... I can't be sure, can I? I didn't see anyone."

"Umm-hmm ...?"

Rob didn't know how much to say.

"See here, Mr. Goodrich. I'm a busy person. Lot's worse stuff going on all day long. But, it's not Halloween. You aren't a teenager playing pranks."

"I didn't do this!"

"All right, but I believe you know who did and what it's all about. And, if we don't stop this now, it could get worse. This is just the start. We don't want this person who has a grudge to get bolder, do we?"

Rob drew in a deep breath and blew it out.

"Think about your family. You have parents?"

"Yeah, Mom and Dad."

"Okay, brothers, sisters?" She watched him closely for his reaction.

"One sister."

"I see. Is this about your sister?"

Rob looked up sharply and dropped his mouth open.

"Your sister then. Tell me. Did your sister do this?" The officer was fishing.

"Absolutely not!" Rob exclaimed.

"And then, it was about your sister," Officer McGillicuddy stated. This guy was easy. His face gave him away. She placed her hand on his arm. "All right, Rob. We've got time. You are going to sit right down and tell me what happened with your sister and this guy who has a grudge." She took his hand. "Come along with me," she said and led him over to the cruiser. She opened her door and invited him in. "You sit right here in the driver's seat, and I'll go around."

Rob took the door handle and waited, in astonishment, to see what she would do. McGillicuddy walked around to the other side, opened the door and took the passenger seat. "Get in," she invited.

With some reluctance, Rob got into the driver's seat. His face must have registered his concern. "What for?" he asked.

"We're not going anywhere," she assured him. "See, I've got the keys." She reached up and turned off the communicator. "No one is listening. Now, tell me about it." She had dropped the cool demeanor and was all warm and inviting, now–his best friend.

"Uh."

"Off the record, Mr. Goodrich. May I call you Robert?"

"It's Rob."

"Okay Rob, I'm all ears." She smiled.

"Um, well …" Rob looked around as if to make sure everything was turned off, "there is a guy who dated my sister. She's only sixteen and he's older. He got fresh with her and she ran into the house. Now he is spreading lies about her all over town. Well, he was until …"

"Until you decided to do something about it," she nodded sympathetically, as if it was all right.

"Maybe I did, maybe I didn't," he grinned sheepishly. Rob wasn't going to admit anything to a cop.

"And now this person who was spreading lies about your sister is paying you back, I see," McGillicuddy surmised.

Rob was silent.

"You see, Rob, that wasn't so hard, was it?"

Rob shrugged.

"Now, all I need to know is: tell me about this person who was dating your sister."

"Just once."

"Okay, I see he dated your sister only one time. The name?"

"I'm not accusing this guy of doing anything."

"Of course, not, I understand. All you know is that he dated your sister."

"Yeah."

"And then he said some unkind things about her."

"Well, more than that. He wrote them on the wall."

"Ah, not just libel. Slander."

"Jeff Totten," said Rob. "Jeff Totten is his name."

"So you think Jeff Totten, who libeled and slandered your sister, also did this to your car and your parents' house?"

"I don't have any way of knowing who did this. I'm just answering your questions."

"That's good enough, Rob. You did the right thing. At this point, Mr. Totten is just a person of interest. Nothing more."

"Thank you, Officer McGillicuddy."

"It's Sharon." She gave a half-smile, for the first time.

"Thank you very much, Sharon," said Rob with a full smile. He glanced at her left hand, looking for a ring. It was bare.

"You are free to leave, Mr. Goodrich," she said, resuming her professional demeanor. "We will file a report for the insurance company."

"Is that all?" Rob asked.

Without a word, Sharon opened her door and exited from the car. She walked around and held the door open for Rob. He stood and remained facing her.

"Goodbye, Mr. Goodrich," she said.

"May I call you?" he asked.

"Sorry, I have to get back on duty," she motioned him aside.

Rob hesitated and then turned up the walk. Sharon McGillicuddy entered her car, sighed and turned on the communicator. "Officer McGillicuddy to dispatch."

"Dispatch. Go ahead."

"Investigation completed," she smiled to herself. "Reporting for duty."

Chapter 5 Airline Flight

*N*ate walked directly to the gate pulling his carry-on case and holding a fake leather briefcase under his arm. Today his old cloth case was in his checked bag, as were his slacks, knit top and jacket from yesterday. His timing was perfect, as usual. He would arrive at the gate with about ten minutes to spare—just enough time to look over the crowd—but not so much that he would stand out, one way or another.

He wore jeans, non-descript walking shoes, and a plain tan sport coat. Whenever Nate was out in public he spent all his time scanning faces, bodies and demeanors, constantly comparing body types, mannerisms, voices and sharpening his powers of observation.

In addition to memorizing names, faces and descriptions, his homework included videos of persons on the watch list. The video could have been shot from any angle and could show the person moving, sometimes talking and laughing. Nate found this sort of study more helpful than mere mug shots, which were taken straight-on and still. When a person was behaving normally, he could give himself away with little "tells" even if wearing a disguise. Sometimes Nate would spend an evening just studying one aspect of people, ears, for instance, or hands. People could change their hair color, paste on facial hair and put lifts in their shoes, gain or lose weight, but they seldom bothered to change their hands, ears and voice.

Nate mulled over the directive he had received just this morning. Homeland Security had become aware of al Qaeda's latest plans to sabotage an American airliner. At first it seemed preposterous, but, of course, al Qaeda was patient. They had gone to great lengths over a period of many months plotting and planning their 9/11 attack. At the time, no one could have predicted what actually happened.

And so now, the current plans seemed equally as incredible. Homeland Security was warning that al Qaeda affiliates planned to sabotage airliners before they even came off the production line. How on earth they could do that baffled Nate. But, the working theory seemed to be that they had spies within the actual manufacturing company who had devised an ingenious plan to plant tiny devices within the planes that would respond to remote control commands. Months or years later, al Qaeda operatives would then be able to sabotage the planes by interfering with the actual electronic control mechanisms while the plane was in flight.

When Nate considered all the redundancies, checks, double checks and triple checks that go into every airplane, he had no idea how this could be done. But, Nate sure didn't want to be flying on any plane that was rigged by al Qaeda—no way! And so, he was taking this seriously. Somehow, al Qaeda was attempting to get operatives actually inside the engineering departments and the top central offices of the largest aviation government contractor in the world.

~~~~~

Old Papers in a Lockbox

Sally let herself into her simple apartment in Arlington, Virginia, hung up her uniform jacket and kicked off her shoes. She would remove the rest of her flight attendant's uniform in a minute, but she was too tired at the moment. Sally grabbed the mail and sat down in the first chair to glance at it. Nothing much here, just junk mail and bills. That was a relief. She dreaded getting those special letters from the agency. This meant she could relax for the evening and not have to go out for a meeting.

She might as well hang up these clothes and get into something comfortable for the evening. But first she took a prepared meal out of the small freezer compartment and set it in the microwave/oven combo to thaw and cook. Twenty minutes later she was showered and dressed in a lounging outfit with a towel wrapped around her wet hair and scuffs on her feet. Savory odors were coming from the tiny kitchen area. Sally's stomach growled. She was starved.

But, first she wanted to get something out of the closet. She pulled a chair over and climbed up. Tall as she was, she couldn't quite reach the lock box tucked away on the highest shelf. She would look inside later and so she carried it with her into the kitchen and set it on the small counter space. Sally grabbed utensils, napkins and set them on a tray along with the dinner. She added bottled water, carried it all into the living area and placed it on a tiny table next to her only comfortable chair.

Sally gingerly lifted one corner of the covering to allow steam to escape before she removed the cover entirely. *Mmm*, she sniffed, closed her eyes and breathed her prayers of thanks, before she set to eating her meal.

Dinner over, it was time to dig through the things in that locked box. It contained her important papers, diplomas, licenses, certifications, warranties, and her birth certificate. It was this latter document that Sally wanted to examine. How many years had it been since she looked at it, if ever? Maybe never, actually. Sally took the paper and set it under a strong light. From a tiny desk, she pulled out a magnifying glass, determined to look at every item and mark. What could she learn here?

Her date of birth was exactly right, twenty-one years ago, this month. The document was signed by a J.M Yarnoka, M.D. Father's name, unknown. Mother's name, Ferrell Millican and her date of birth was right, but the place of birth was Portland, Oregon. That was interesting. Where did Sally get the impression that Ferrell was a Canadian citizen? In fact, there was nothing here that indicated either Sally or her mother had dual citizenship in the US and Canada—another misconception. Of course, Ferrell could have immigrated to Canada, in which case she would have given up her US citizenship. Or, maybe she was born in Canada and immigrated to the US. Who knows? Where were Ferrell's important papers? Sally wondered. There was so much that she didn't know.

Sally picked up the magnifying glass and looked at each word and mark carefully. Wait a minute-what was this? Sally looked more closely at the i's and e's. She pulled the light even closer. Could there be some mistake? It looked as if Sally's last name was not the same as her mother's—Millecan and Millican. She examined them again. Then she noticed the c in Millecan. The side was straighter than it should be and the bottom part of the c wasn't quite right. Sally compared it with another c in a different place on the document. They were different! And then she noticed that the a was different, as well. She held the paper up to the light to backlight the paper. She was able to see some tiny scratch marks. Sally's heart beat faster. Her mother's words came back to her, *You're not my daughter. I know my own daughter. Her name is Sally Miller.*

Sally picked up the magnifying glass and examined the name again. Could it have been Miller, originally, and then changed to Millecan? A shock of electricity went down her spine and a wave of fear settled around her like a shroud. What did this mean? Would she ever know the truth? Did she really want to know? Of course she did, didn't she?

Questions swirled around in her mind throughout the night, until she willed herself to sleep. Tomorrow was a new day. Things always looked better in the morning.

Besides she had a date and now a place of birth. It was a simple matter to call the County Courthouse and order a new birth certificate. The official records had to be right. Didn't they?

~~~~~

At the Totten Residence--the Investigation

Judge Totten frowned at the uniformed officer who rang his doorbell. The judge drew up to his full height and looked down his nose. "Good evening, officer," he said.

"Good evening, sir," replied Officer McGillicuddy. "May I come in?"

"That depends," said the judge. "Is this an official visit?'

"Yessir," said McGillicuddy.

"And what is the nature of your call," his tone had cooled, "if you please?"

"I would like to have a word with Mr. Jeff Totten. Is he at home?"

"Jeff is my son."

"May I come in?"

"Do you have a warrant?" he demanded.

"No sir. This is just an investigation. We have a few questions of your son."

"Is he wanted for some kind of crime?"

"No sir, we just have a few questions."

"What is this about?"

"We will discuss that with Mr. Jeff Totten, sir." With an emphasis on the sir, Sharon allowed a professional chill in her voice. "Is he at home?"

"Do you know who I am?" Judge Totten was getting a bit huffy in an effort to intimidate the lessor person—lessor in his view, that is.

Sharon remained unruffled. "According to your statement, sir, you are the father of Mr. Jeff Totten, the person to whom we wish to speak."

"Harummph, I'll have you know, young lady, that I am Judge Totten, an officer of the Court," he said, indignantly.

"Thank you, Judge Totten. And now, If I may come in, I need to speak with your son." Sharon was not the least bit cowed by this arrogant personage. She would be polite, but firm.

"I'm afraid I cannot allow that."

"I see. Are you certain, sir? Perhaps it would be wiser if I had a quiet conversation with your son, here, rather than have him arrested and taken to police headquarters. Don't you agree?"

"That's preposterous!"

"Do you really think so?" asked Sharon calmly.

"There is not another judge in this town who would dare to issue a warrant …"

"Who's at the door, Norville?" a young female voice interrupted.

"It's no one, dear," called the judge.

"What did you say, honey?"

"No one!" he said, louder.

Sharon said nothing, waiting to see how this developed.

"Well, then will you please close the door? I feel a draft."

"Oh dammit, come in and close the door, but don't you take a step further," he growled at Sharon, who was enjoying this domestic scene immensely. It appeared that the big haughty self-important judge was just a pussycat around his little woman.

"Thank you, sweetie," called Mrs. Totten. "I just got out of the shower. You wouldn't want your date for the evening to catch her death, would you?"

Sharon had all she could do to keep a straight face. At that point a young man came racing down the open staircase, almost bumping into Sharon. "Oh! Excuse me. I didn't see you there, officer." He stopped abruptly, and looked from his dad to Sharon. "Ugh, am I interrupting?" he asked, lamely.

Sharon stepped in front of the man, blocking him from the judge. "Are you Jeff Totten?" she asked, directly in his face.

"Yes," he answered, and began to turn pink.

"I have a few questions for you Mr. Totten in connection with an investigation."

"Dad?" Jeff appealed craning his neck around the officer.

The judge was rooted to his spot. Mrs. Totten—a lovely younger woman—came up and stood beside the judge, dressed in a bathrobe with bare feet and a towel wrapped around her head. "What's going on?" she asked.

"Shh," said the judge.

"Where were you on Monday evening, two days ago?" asked McGillicuddy, speaking to the younger man.

"W-well, I was right here all evening."

"And all night, as well? Did you leave the house at any time during the evening or night?"

"N-no," Jeff said, shaking his head.

"That's not true, Jeff," his mother chimed in. "I heard you go out about midnight. We were already in bed."

"Shh," said the judge. "Be quiet." He tried to shush her up.

Sharon looked at Jeff, steadily, "Your mother remembers something different, Mr. Totten."

"Well, now I recall. Yes, I did go out for a little while."

"I see. And where did you go?"

"I … I went to the store … yes, that's what I did … I went to the store."

"What store was that?"

"A grocery store."

"At that time of night?"

"It was an all-night grocery store."

"I'm sure you remember which store."

Jeff nodded, "Yeah."

"And what did you buy?"

"I don't remember."

"Did you buy some eggs?"

"No."

"No doubt you can tell us what store and what you bought. You might even have the sales slip still in the bag or in a trash can. It would probably have the time on it as well, which would corroborate with the records at the store, don't you agree? There aren't too many customers at that time of night."

"I probably threw it away."

"That's too bad, Mr. Totten, because we would like to clear you of any possible involvement in an incident that took place at that time on the other side of town."

"What is the meaning of this?" roared the judge. "Are you accusing my son of a crime? Don't say another word, Jeff."

Jeff looked from his father to the policewoman. "Uh … well, maybe I did buy a few eggs," he admitted under his breath, "but that's no crime."

"Thank you, Jeff," Sharon praised him.

"It is good to be honest with a police officer," said Mrs. Totten. "You did the right thing, son."

Jeff started to wring his hands. "Is that all, officer? I need to get going." He started to walk away.

"Just one more thing, Jeff. I presume you still have the eggs you bought?"

Jeff looked from his mom to his dad for help.

"Don't answer her," said the judge, raising his voice.

"What do you mean, don't answer her," argued the mother. "Jeff is a good boy. He will cooperate with the police. Answer the question, Jeff. My goodness. Let's get this over with. I'm getting ready to go out." She pulled her robe closer around her.

Jeff said nothing.

Sharon spoke, "There is no crime in buying eggs, unless you use them for a nefarious purpose."

"What do you mean?" asked the judge.

"Vandalism," she answered.

"Of what sort?"

Sharon turned to Jeff. "It appears that someone threw more than a few dozen eggs at a car and at a brick house, causing a mess, which will result in monetary damages. As you know this sort of thing can cost a lot to have professionally cleaned. It will probably require steam cleaning and pressure washing. We don't know whether there will be permanent damage to the finish."

"Oh dear," said Mrs. Totten, as she sank into a chair and began to fan herself.

"Did you do this childish thing?" demanded the judge, walking toward his son.

"I didn't mean any harm. I was just getting even."

"Go to your room," the judge ordered, as if Jeff was still a little boy.

Jeff slunk halfway up the stairs and turned, his head bowed.

"Whatever it costs, we will pay double the damages," said the exasperated judge. "Provided, of course, that the complaint is dropped and there is a non-disclosure agreement." He moved to the front door and held it open. "Thank you very much, officer. My lawyer will be in touch." He appeared to be dismissing her.

"I will make my report, sir. It will be up to the offended party as to whether they wish to press charges. Good evening, Mrs. Totten. Jeff. Judge," she nodded at each one and left.

Smiling, Sharon paused outside the door for a moment listening to the raised voices on the other side.

Mission accomplished.

Chapter 6 Reagan International

$\mathcal{E}$ ven though it was summertime, normally hot in the capital city, the air was a bit nippy at this early hour. Sally Millecan, or Miller, whichever, had an eleven o'clock departure at Reagan International, but she had to arise early to meet with her lobbyist contact at 8:00 AM. Why at that hour, she did not know. They paid her well and never told her anything.

Darn, she hated this, but it had to be done. Sometimes she wished she could get out of this mess. But, it was a responsibility that was thrust upon her and not of her choice. At least it was interesting.

The message had indicated the contact person was willing to meet at the airport. That helped. Sally grabbed a tray and moved down the cafeteria line, picking up a few items from the breakfast offerings. She selected an outside table near the entrance, so that her contact could find her. It was a strange and different person sometimes, so all Sally could do was wait the half hour allowed for this visit.

Sally started in on her breakfast. No telling when the person would arrive and who it would be. Finishing her food, she kept her eye on the time. If the contact didn't show up, that wasn't Sally's problem, so long as they paid her, of course.

Clearing the table and refilling her coffee cup, Sally glanced at her watch. She would give it another ten minutes and then she had work to do.

No one showed, and so Sally reached for her things and started to rise. Just then a teenage girl, dressed in jeans and a crop-top, ran up and pulled out the other chair. Breathlessly, she spoke, "Sorry I'm late."

Sally resumed her seat.

"Hello, Sally." The girl grinned and greeted Sally as if they were old pals. Her chest heaving, she continued, "Washington traffic. I ran all the way from the cab stand."

Sally glanced at her watch, "You are so late, I only have a minute."

"This won't take long," said the girl. "Your instructions are to locate and make friends with this man." She shoved a picture at Sally. "The description is on the back."

Sally picked up the picture, studied it for a moment and turned it over to read the back. It wasn't one of her regulars.

"I'll take that," said the girl removing the picture from Sally's hand.

"Let me see that again," said Sally.

"All right, for just a few moments. Memorize the details quickly, I have to leave."

Sally concentrated on the picture and details. "Do you have his name?"

"No, you are to learn that, and report. Do not lose contact with him. Get close to him. You know how."

"Why?" asked Sally.

"That is all I know." The girl grabbed the picture and ran off without another word.

Amazed, Sally shook her head. *Well ... okee-dokee. I guess I can handle that,* she thought. *Onward to the next chapter in this crazy day.*

Sally's 11:43 AM flight was out of Reagan into Dallas Love Field. Flight #1715 , DCA to DAL was actually on Virgin America airlines, which was a partner of Alaska Air. It was a bit unusual for her to work a Virgin Air flight, but they were short-handed and she agreed to do it for a friend. Besides she would pick up extra money for that leg, double-duty actually. The itinerary changed planes in Dallas onto an Alaska Air flight #3379 continuing on to Seattle-Tacoma International, landing there at 5:42 PM. It was the only Alaska Air Flight of many out of DC to SEA-TAC that stopped in Dallas. As such, it was a popular one for folks doing business or having interest in the huge airline company, because Dallas was the World Headquarters of their international trade. The company had offices in over 300 cities and did business with many countries, not just in airplanes, but in all sorts of technology, military hardware, space hardware and top-secret designs.

This would be a long day for Sally. Although it did not sound long because of the changing time zones, it was actually nine hours

~~~~~

Greeting the captain, crew, fellow flight attendants and boarding passengers kept Sally busy and her mind occupied for the next hour or two. Serving the first-class passengers left little spare time. The first break came after lunch was served. Sally leaned against a bulkhead and rested while her guests were busy eating. It was only when she had a chance to revisit her "part-time" assignment for the day that she allowed her eyes to roam over the passengers wondering which one fit the picture. This was not easy. Too many of them were middle-aged business men. Sometimes they all looked alike. Sally wished there had been one distinguishing feature that would set the target person apart from the rest. But, maybe that was the point. The subject had no distinguishing features. That is what made him perfect. Whatever made him special was just exactly nothing.

Sally struggled to remember what was on the front and back of the man's picture—middle-aged, medium height and build, round face, slightly receding hairline, moderate complexion, medium voice, no jewelry, drinks coffee black, no other distinguishing features. *Come now!* thought Sally. *Takes his coffee black? That's all? Give me a break. Well, okay, I'll just have to use the process of elimination.*

She started sighting down the aisle, eyeing each business man. Some she already knew. Guessing their ages, she sorted out several more for being too young or too old. Concentrating on those remaining, she rejected them, one at a time. Either they wore jewelry, were too short, tall or fat, had long faces, no hair, or too much hair. That left just three to consider. She gazed at each one in turn, comparing them to the picture in her mind's eye. She was stumped. It could be any one of the three.

Pondering what to do, she had an idea—maybe the voices and coffee would give them away. Picking up the coffee pot she moved down the aisle, pausing to offer refills, making a point to look each of her three candidates in the face, if possible. Speaking directly at the first candidate, she smiled and said, "May I refill your coffee, sir?"

"No thank you," he said in a low bass voice.

Sally mentally crossed him off the list.

The second candidate shook his head no. Sally had to think quickly to get him to say something. "Is there anything else you need?

He held up his cup for a refill and nodded.

Sally noticed that he used creamer in his coffee, but she needed to be sure. "Are you enjoying your meal?" she tried again.

"Good," he said in a deep voice. Just one word, but it was enough for her to smile and move on to the last possibility. When she approached this man's seat she noticed that he became busy reaching down under the seat for something— whatever he had placed down there.

"Excuse me, sir," she said, "May I refill your coffee?"

He shook his head and continued to look down, away from her.

"All right, sir," she said. "Just push that call button up here, if you need anything." She hoped he would look up at the call button, but he only murmured, "Mm-mm," and nodded.

The voice sounded medium, but she couldn't be sure. Sally noticed that he drank his coffee black. Maybe this was the only clue she would get. Sally sighed and moved on to serve the others. This was turning out to be more difficult than she expected. Maybe she would not get close to this man, at all. All she knew, so far, was his name on the passenger list, George

F. George. Well, that was a start, if it was a real name it certainly was a distinguishing feature.

From time to time, for the rest of the flight, Sally used her short breaks to pull out her cell phone and surreptitiously take pictures of the three passengers whom she had originally identified. Mr. George F. George turned out to be impossible to photograph. He kept his head down most of the time. When he finally fell asleep for a nap, Sally thought she got a couple of shots, but they turned out to be useless. It was only after they landed in Dallas that Sally was able to get a video of his retreating back as he left the plane.

At this point she had to put the phone away lest other folks notice. In fact one of the other crew members asked her what was going on. "Are you having trouble, Sally?" she asked. "I noticed you on the phone a lot."

"Thanks for asking," Sally smiled back and tried to cover up. "No, nothing like that." she shrugged and got busy with something in the galley.

Mr. George was stopping here, not continuing on to Seattle, and so there was nothing more to do. Sally would make her report and forget it. It was one of her frustrations and typical of her assignments for the lobbyist group. There was never any follow-up. It was as if her reports simply disappeared into a black hole. If it were not for the good money, she would ditch this job, as there seemed to be very little work resulting in accomplishing anything.

~~~~~

Run-Around

Miles away, Rob Goodrich was experiencing similar emotions. He hadn't been able to learn anything about the vandalism complaint. His calls to the police department ended in frustration, pretty much receiving the run-around. They were in the business of not telling victims anything about a "so-called" ongoing investigation. They used that excuse to operate on a closed circuit. Truthfully, Rob doubted they were doing anything.

He reasoned, *"Maybe the problem might be that I just need to show up in person."* And so, he paid a visit to the local police station. At the front desk, he shifted from one foot to the other for several minutes before someone bothered to wait on him. No one seemed to be in any hurry as they sauntered from file cabinet to desk, to computer and back to a file cabinet. Rob made some noise, he cleared his throat and tried to catch someone's eye. It was amazing how people seemed to go about their activities as if the front desk wasn't even there. Finally, he spoke up, "Er … excuse me," he began. Only one person on the far side of the room looked up at him and then right back at the papers he was studying. Rob tried again, "Hello, is anyone helping here?"

"Good afternoon," one clerk greeted him from across the room, "There is no one at the desk right now. We're short-handed today."

"B-but, I'm looking for Officer McGillicuddy," Rob stammered. "Is she in?"

"I'm new here," the clerk shrugged and turned away

"But, isn't there anyone who can help me?"

No one answered.

Rob opened his arms wide and shook his head, "I can't believe this!" he said in a loud voice. A couple people looked up without saying anything. Another person yawned.

By no means defeated, Rob turned and slammed out of the precinct station. *What next?* he wondered. Well, I guess I could get back and spend some time checking on my car.

He had driven it down to a car restoration place, which happened to be downtown, only a few blocks from the police station. Having jogged over to the station, he would walk back. At least those people were helpful. *I guess it makes a difference when they are getting paid to keep the customers happy.* It would take about half an hour for the people to make an evaluation on the cleanup project for Rob's car. The estimator had walked around the car, going "tsk-tsk" and shaking his head. "Yup," he concluded, "it's eggs all right. We don't usually get these until Halloween. Gonna take some time." He lifted the hood and peered inside. "Hmm," he chewed on his cigar. "Might have to do a steam-clean in here."

"What's that going to cost?" Rob asked.

"Can't say for sure," said the man, "Depends."

"What do you mean?"

"Haf-ta' put it up on the hoist. See what's underneath."

"How long will that take?"

"Maybe thirty-forty minutes. Ain't ya got something to do? Go see your girl and come back. I'll have an estimate all wrote up for ya'."

So, Rob had gone to see his girl, not that she was really his girl. No matter, that hadn't worked out so well.

Back at the car restoration agency, he walked in and braced himself for the bad news.

A woman looked up from the cash register. "Good afternoon, may I help you?"

"Robert Goodrich. I'm here to get the estimate on my car."

"Yes, of course, Mr. Goodrich. I have it right here." She leafed through a stack of papers and pulled out a computer printout nicely done in triplicate. "Here you are, sir."

Rob picked it up and began reading down a list of items. He had no idea how complicated such a clean-up would be. Each item had a number, name, time required and price tag. Bottom line, $569.99. A small whistle escaped through his teeth.

"Is everything all right?" asked the clerk.

"Oh sure, this is fine ... I guess." He let his voice fall.

"Scott's Body Shop does a fantastic and thorough job, Mr. Goodrich. You can be confident that your car will look, feel and smell as if it just rolled out of the showroom. Shall I schedule the work?"

"Well, I'm wondering whether I should run this by my insurance company."

"That is perfectly permitted, Mr. Goodrich, but I can assure you we are the very best in town, sometimes the only one in town for certain problems and conditions."

"Thanks, I'll get back to you," said Rob, thinking *I may have one of those conditions.*

"In the meantime, can you drive your car?"

"Well, yes I drove it down here, but I couldn't see out of all the windows. I had to scrape the windshield off as best I could."

"Um, I see. Well, then maybe it isn't safe for you to be driving it very far."

"I suppose you're right."

"Perhaps you could phone your insurance adjuster from here."

"I'll do that. May I use your phone?"

"Yes, sir. I'll show you into the lounge." She led him down a short hall and into a visitor's lounge.

No wonder the estimate is so high, Rob thought. *This is some fancy place.*

"You will be comfortable right in here, sir. Use the phone on the desk. I think you will find everything you need, computers, television, video games, and refreshments in the mini-kitchen over there."

"Thank you," said Rob and blew out a breath, ready to get busy and accomplish something.

Chapter 7 Eyes on Alert

$\mathcal{T}$his was his third and last flight of the day. Nate seldom had more than two, unless they were really short flights. This evening flight would be a forty-five minute hop across Lake Michigan into Chicago—no big deal. Flying into the setting sun would be beautiful.

After four days on the road, he was tired, ready to get settled down for the night and fly home tomorrow. One nice thing about this job was that he would have four days off ... well ... only three if you don't count the partial day he would spend flying home. It was unusual to have his last flight be close enough that he could fly home that same day.

Tomorrow's flight home would take most of the day by the time he waited in line, checked in, boarded, and flew coach just like any other passenger. Off-duty meant there was no telling what seat he would have.

Nate took his seat on the aisle and fastened his seat belt. This would be a "dry" flight, no drinks, no food, not even a peanut. There was no time for such service. Between the time spent getting up to altitude and then descending into O'Hare, there was no more than fifteen or twenty minutes at cruising altitude. For the most part passengers stayed in their seats.

Nate was seated in coach just behind the first-class section and very close to the front of the plane. And so once the seat belt sign was switched off, he immediately got up and slowly walked back to the lavatory. There was one man in 14B whom he wanted to see again.

Earlier, Nate had noticed this man in the holding area. There was something about him that Nate didn't like, something in his downturned eyes and the way he seemed to move his hands.

They were never still. His dress shoes did not fit with the blue jeans he wore. Most people wore sneakers with jeans. Also, the jeans were brand new and seemed ill-fitting. Small details, of course, but they caught Nate's attention. He had gone so far as to follow the man to the men's room to watch his gait and mannerisms.

Nate had had a gut feeling about the guy. Something didn't add up. He had moved closer to where the man was seated in order to observe him, and then positioned himself behind the man when they waited in line to board. Nate was able to study his mannerisms and catch a glimpse of the man's rather odd name.

Nate slowly walked the full length of the aisle again. This time he stopped at his own seat to sit for a minute to quietly retrieve his backpack from under the seat in front of him. Nate wanted to hold this close for the rest of the flight.

Once again he moved to the back of the plane, this time with his back-pack in hand. Entering the lavatory, he removed his high-tech weapons from the pack, placing one in his pocket, one in his belt and two throwing knives in his boots. Plastic handcuffing devices were already in his left pocket. He left the lavatory and casually leaned up against the back wall with no plans to move until this plane was safely on the ground.

Perhaps nothing would happen, but he was on guard.

Ten minutes passed. Nate could see Lake Michigan down below. Soon the pilots would request permission to begin their descent into O'Hare. Nate could imagine the communication that was now going on between the co-pilot and the in-route controller.

"United Flight 302 to Control, requesting permission to descend to 10,000 feet."

Nate's eye roamed over the passengers, back and forth over seat 14B. The air was bumpier at this lower altitude. He expected the seat belt sign to flash on momentarily.

Suddenly the man in 14B rose from his seat and lurched toward the front of the plane, hanging onto seat backs to steady himself. Nate was up the aisle in a flash, directly behind the man who pulled back the curtain to the first-class section and opened the lavatory door.

Nate held him back with a strong hold of the man's arm. "Sir, excuse me," said Nate. "This is the first-class section. Your lavatory is in the back."

"What?" He tried to jerk away. "Oh … sorry," said the man.

"In the back." Nate spoke quietly, while pulling on the arm.

Just then the seat belt sign came on, along with the pilot's voice. "Please take your seats and fasten your seat-belts. We will be landing in Chicago in ten minutes."

Two flight attendants moved up. "Sirs, you need to take your seats."

The man looked at the attendant, "I'll only be a minute."

"No sir, you need to take your seat," the hostess insisted.

"Can I sit here, please?" he asked, pointing at an empty seat in first class.

Nate stayed close and did not let go of the man. What would they say? What would they do? Was this man dangerous, or simply confused and misguided? Nate had to know. Already he could feel the plane turn, preparing to line up for the runway.

He and the man both swayed as the wheels descended causing a slight shake and rumbling noise. Nate pretended to lose his balance. He bumped up against the man and quickly felt him for weapons. Nothing. But wait … there was an odd shape in the coal pocket. Nate quickly removed it from the man's pocket and slipped it into his own. His grip tightened on the man, at the same time as his eyes constantly surveyed the plane for any other disturbances. He did not expect these people to operate alone.

"Sirs, please, take your seats," pleaded the flight attendant.

"Thank you," said Nate. "We will sit right here." He moved the man into the closest seat and hastily sat beside him. Nate buckled the man in and then buckled himself. The runway was in sight, the airplane on approach. It was too late to move the two men.

The captain announced, "Flight attendants, please take your seats." They lowered the small seats from the wall, for just this purpose and belted themselves in just as the airplane's wheels touched the runway. Immediately the engines reversed thrust and roared to slow the plane, which bucked like a wild stallion ridden for the first time. Nate braced himself against the g-forces, throwing an arm in front of the man, as if to hold him, while feeling of his chest for hidden devices.

In two minutes the airplane was gliding smoothly down the runway. The second they turned off the runway onto the taxiway, Nate pulled out his cell phone and typed an emergency message to the O'Hare branch of the Air Marshal Service. "Arrest emerging passenger, George F. George, on suspicion. Arriving Terminal 1, Gate C6, United Flight 302. Photo to follow," and signed it with his badge number.

Nate held up his phone as if to take a selfie, with the camera lens pointed directly at Mr. George. "Look here, George. What do you think this is?" Before he caught himself, George glanced up and then quickly covered his face. In that instant Nate snapped his picture and clicked Send.

George tried to grab the camera. "No, no picture," he cried.

Nate moved the phone slightly and took his own picture. "See?" he said, showing the picture to George. "It's only me. No problem." He slid the phone into his pocket with an innocent looking grin. "Clever gadget, these phones," he said and continued to gaze at the window, watching G. F. George out the corner of his eye, as they glided up to the terminal.

As soon as they were at the gate, passengers filled the aisle, pulling their belongings from under the seats and out of the overhead bins. Nate sat back and gazed out the window as Mr. George crowded toward the door, wanting to be among the first to depart. Oddly enough, he did not have any luggage with him, not even a small case. Or if he did, he was leaving it behind in his haste to get out of there.

Nate waited until most of the passengers had left. It gave him time to carefully examine each one who passed by. He was interested to see if anyone acted strangely. Nate would capture their picture for later comparison. He was confident that other Federal Air Marshals were right now arresting Mr. George and watching all the other passengers as they disembarked.

It would behoove Nate to behave just like any other Chicago native, coming home. He would disappear in order to protect his identity as Mr. N. Mavis from the suburb of Highland Park. No one except Nate's immediate superior would know that he had disarmed a passenger and prevented a possible attack.

After the passengers had cleared the aisle, Nate moved back to his original seat to retrieve his carry-on bag from the overhead. He examined seat 14B, underneath and overhead to see if G. F. George had left anything behind. Nothing was there. Nevertheless, Nate pulled opened the literature pocket for a thorough check. Ah ... here was a paperback novel someone had left behind. Nate wrapped it in a handkerchief and put it into his back-pack. Shouldering the pack, he wheeled his bag down the aisle and off the plane.

Walking up the ramp, he reached into the inside pocket of his jacket and donned a pair of colored glasses with striking-looking rims. He removed his jacket, quickly folded it and slipped it into a side pocket of his bag. Underneath he wore a brightly patterned sweater that looked nothing like the drab jacket he wore all during the flight. These changes were small, but could be enough to prevent his being noticed as the one who stood by Mr. George. Stopping off in the men's room at the concourse he attached some fake facial hair, changed shoes and put on gloves.

Taking his time to walk to the carousel, his bag would have already come down. Thus more than half the passengers had left. Nate did not want to stand around. He could grab his bag and leave. Without stopping he walked quickly to the taxicab stand and entered the first one in line. He knew where he wanted to go, to a classy downtown hotel where he could take in a first-class show. Instead, this time he opted for the good old Holiday Inn Embassy Suites.

First he wanted to pick up dinner. Watching the restaurants go by out the window he chose one on the right. "I'll pick up some Kentucky Fried Chicken," he directed the cabbie. "Please take me through the drive-up." The driver complied, pausing at the ordering station. As Nate slid over and rolled down the back window he asked the cab driver, "Can I order anything for you?"

"I could sure use a grilled chicken sandwich and medium black coffee," the man replied.

"Will do," said Nate. He placed the order, adding a regular chicken dinner for himself. "Please put them in separate bags," he instructed.

"I'll subtract my order from your tab," offered the cabbie.

"Not at all. My treat," said Nate. Normally he would not do this as it would call attention to himself, but, in this case, he could hardly do otherwise. He hoped his largesse would not come back to haunt him. Sometimes one mistake was all it took to seal your doom.

He paid at the takeout window, accepted his change and handed the cabbie his food.

"Gee thanks," said the cabbie.

"You're welcome."

As a precaution, Nate rode slumped down in his seat, making himself invisible from the outside. Five minutes later they drew up to the Inn. Nate quickly paid the driver, gathered his things and entered the front door in less than a minute. This time he handled his own luggage, moved up to the desk and gave the clerk a second identity. He was no longer Mr. N. Mavis.

"Good evening Mr. Sheldon," said the desk clerk. "We have a king-size suite on the fourth floor available. Will that do?"

"Yes, perfect," said Nate.

The clerk swiped Nate's credit card, and handed it back along with a key and a newspaper. "Breakfast is served starting at six. Will that be soon enough for you?"

"Yes, thank you. Good-night," said Nate as he turned toward the elevator.

Already a mysterious man known only as J.M.–Mr. George's secret control–was following Nate's trail. He was determined to discover who this N. Mavis could be who so effectively sabotaged the plan to take down a passenger plane and dump it into Lake Michigan. J.M. suspected he was some kind of federal agent, maybe even military. Mavis was too slick to be a mere cop or bodyguard. J.M. had jumped into the second taxi in line and ordered the driver to follow Nate's cab. He was able to get the cab number and a good look at Nate's driver and would question him later. Probably it would require a bribe and a good story to get the cab driver to talk. But, it was essential to hurry and neutralize Mavis before he had a chance to report to authorities.

J.M. had no idea what Mavis knew, but he couldn't leave any loose ends. He would take care of Mavis before morning, maybe even within the hour.

When Nate's taxi pulled in at the KFC restaurant, J.M. was confused. He no longer saw the passenger. Did he make a mistake, following the wrong cab? He saw the driver place what appeared to be a take-out coffee mug up to his lips, and then bite down on a sandwich. What the hell was going on? Did Mavis give him the slip?

J.M. ordered his driver to take him back to the KFC place. "Just pull in and let me out here," he ordered. J.M. ran into the restaurant and began a hurried search of the entire place, including every stall in the men's room. For a second he peeked in the women's room and wondered, *should I go in there? Maybe later.* For now he ran outside and circled all the way around the parking lot and nearby street and sidewalk.

Just then a city bus pulled away from the curb and entered traffic. *Damn, Mavis must have gotten on the bus!* J.M. could sprint for short distances. He took off after the bus, hoping to catch up with it at the next stop. Heavy traffic might slow the bus. Too late, the bus slowed at the next corner and kept going. His heart pounding, chest heaving, J.M. had to stop. Mavis may have gotten away this time, but there was still the first cabbie.

J.M. waited at the bus stop, hoping to flag down a cab. He had perfected the loudest whistle in the service and he used it now. Two cabs saw him but kept on going. The third one pulled to the curb. J.M. open the back door and got in. "Airport," he directed, "and hurry."

He pulled out a large bill and handed it to the driver.

Smiling broadly, the driver grabbed the bill with one hand, wheeled around with the other and headed toward the airport. "Yessiree, Mate. I'll have you there in a flash."

Navigating expertly through the labyrinth that is O'Hare's miles of roadways, the cabbie asked, "Where are you going, mate?"

"Let me off at the United Air baggage claim," said J.M. Realizing that made little sense, J.M. explained. "I didn't pick up my bag." That still made no sense, so he added, "I need to check with the lost baggage people. They seem to have found it."

The cabbie thought this was a bit strange, but he wasn't about to say so. Didn't the guy know that any airlines would deliver his bags to his hotel, home or wherever he was staying? Probably the guy was a foreigner, from the sounds. Being a foreigner himself, that was of little consequence to him.

"Stop right here, please," said J.M. "behind those cabs is good."

The driver pulled into the line of taxicabs waiting their turn for a fare and stopped. J.M. jumped out and moved rapidly up the line of cabs, checking each one for its number. Chances were slim to none he would find Mavis's cabbie this way, but he had to try. It was his only lead. He figured the cabbie would come back here eventually.

A lucky break—halfway up the line he found the identical cab company and numbered cab with the very same driver. He opened the back door and got in.

"Sorry, sir," said the driver. "I'm not allowed to jump ahead in line. Union rules. You have to take the first cab in line."

"Rules are made to be broken," growled J.M. as he held out a large bill. "I just have a few questions and then you can go."

The driver pulled forward, still in line. "Sorry, sir, I have to take the passenger in my turn or I'll lose my license."

"I'll make this quick. Just tell me where you took the guy before you stopped off at the Kentucky Fried Chicken."

"I have no idea what you are talking about. Get out of my cab."

"I think you do," threatened J.M. as he pressed the cold barrel of a 45 automatic into the cabbie's neck.

"Hey, wait a minute. What the hell is going on."

"A simply question, my friend. Where is Mavis?"

"I don't know no Mavis. You want my money?"

"Mavis was wearing a bright colored sweater and slacks, and had a beard and funny looking colored glasses."

"O-oh, t-that guy," said the driver nervously. "Look I don't want n-no t-trouble. I've gotta wife 'n' kids."

J.M. shoved the barrel of the gun harder. "Want to see them again? Answer the question."

"I took 'im to the train station," lied the cabbie, hoping the guy was a stranger in these parts.

"You're lying. You weren't gone long enough to drive to the train station. Did he get out at the Kentucky Fried?"

Sweat poured off the cabbie. Hundreds of people walked by. Couldn't anyone see what was happening?

"No. We just got food there. He wanted food and he bought me a sandwich and coffee."

"That's right, very good," said J.M. jamming the gun again. "Then, where did you drop him off?"

"Okay, I took him to the Holiday Inn. That's the truth."

"Which one?"

"The Suites, Holiday Inn Suites." The cabbie gurgled as the switchblade sliced neatly through his carotid artery. Blood gushed over the front of the cab and his head flopped.

Coolly the passenger wiped the blade, folded it and slipped it back into his jacket pocket along with the gun. He pulled a hat down over his eyes, donned slim leather gloves, slid over to the outside door and slipped out into the traffic. He would not use another cab this night. Instead he would walk forward toward where the hotel vans stop. The Holiday Inn Express shuttle would be by soon.

But, first he needed to look more like a tourist, one with luggage. He ducked into the baggage claim area, away from the areas crowded with incoming passengers and toward darkened areas that had long ago finished disgorging themselves. He walked past one and then another dark and silent carousel until he found just what he needed, an abandoned bag that had been left behind by some careless owner. It sat alone on the carousel, waiting as if it had his name on it. He walked up to the bag and lifted it off, acting pleased as if he had just found his long-lost bag, set it on the floor and began wheeling it off with a smile on his face.

He did not wait long before the Holiday Inn shuttle approached the group of weary traveler's waiting at the curb. "Holiday Inn Express Suites?" he asked. The driver pointed to the sign. J.M. boarded, along with the others, allowing the driver to lift his bag onto the rack.

Approaching the Inn's check-in desk, he said, "Would you please ring Mr. Mavis's room and let him know I'm here?"

"Certainly, sir, and who shall I say is calling?"

"Tell him, it's the cabbie," said J.M.

"And your name?"

"Does that matter?" asked J.M. wishing this stupid broad would stop asking so many dumb questions.

"Sir?"

"Just tell him it's his cab driver. Tell him he left his bag in the cab," He said gesturing toward the bag.

The clerk was trained to watch for strange requests. This man was obviously no cabbie.

"I'll check the guest register, sir. Just one moment."

She clacked away on her keyboard. "I'm sorry, sir, we have no Mavis registered tonight. Did you spell that M-a-v-i-s, or could it be e-s, a-s, o-s, or u-s?" Meanwhile she had pushed a secret button that summoned the manager.

"Yes, I think so, but try them all."

"Yes, sir." She typed some more and then looked up. Shaking her head she said, "I've tried Mavis with the alternate spellings, Davis, Avis, Travis, Marvis and Mattis. Can you think of any other possibility?"

J.M. was fit to be tied. He wanted to strangle the woman. "Let me see your register," he leaned over the counter trying to grab something.

"Sir! You can't come around here."

"Give me the damned register or else!" he shouted.

"We don't have registers, sir. Everything is on the computer these days."

J.M. flew around the counter and roughly shoved the woman away and into the wall. She started screaming and didn't stop. He stepped up to the computer and started pushing buttons. Just then, the manager came out of the back. "What is the meaning of this?" he demanded. "What are you doing." He pulled a cell phone out of his pocket and pushed the emergency button for 911.

Quickly J.M. pulled a gun and aimed at the manager. "Drop it!" he screamed. The manager backed away intending to run. J.M. shot twice. The manager dropped. The girl tried to escape on her hands and knees. J.M. shot her dead. She collapsed in a pool of blood. J.M. quickly turned to the computer. The guest list and rooms assignments were still up on the display. J.M. used the up and down buttons to scroll through the names. There were too many, but none starting with M and none that even came close. Sirens sounded in the distance. With only seconds, he tried to read as many names as he could, hoping against hope to see some clue. Time was running out. He looked around frantically for a room key. He would pretend to be a guest. No, that wouldn't work. He wasn't signed in and would be trapped in a room.

He had to escape quickly. Leaving his bag and gun behind he raced for the back exit. No, it was better to leave by the side door. Cops would be around back soon. He pushed frantically on the door release and fled into the outdoor pool area as the door clicked closed and locked. He could now hear police cars at the front and back of the hotel. He was right about that. J.M. wasted precious seconds looking for a gate. Seeing none, he had no choice but to scale the fence. He got a running start and jumped as high as he could, catching the top with one hand. It was sharp. He did not notice his hand was bleeding. Grasping with both hands, he pulled himself up and got one leg over, ripping his pant-leg. No time left he barreled over the fence, disregarding his arms, legs and clothes. He fell to the ground and ran for his life away from the noise of the sirens.

A block away, he ducked down a driveway and behind a darkened office building. Leaning against a back wall, panting for breath, he tried to think. He had to stay off the main road out of sight, but get as far away from here as possible. It would take time for the cops to search the hotel, and then organize a search of the area. How many minutes, he could only guess. At some point there might be helicopters out scouring the area. But, maybe not. This was Chicago—Murder City, USA. Numerous shootings every night. This would be just one of many. Spread thin as they were, only a few cops would be assigned to this incident, he hoped.

What he did not know was that this area was not in Chicago, but in an affluent suburb with far less crime and its own police force. Also, he did not know that Mr. Sheldon, nee Mavis, nee Nate Goodrich, Federal Air Marshal, was on the crime scene calling in the Feds at this very moment.

Chapter 8 Old Pals Meet Again

"*I*f I'm not still at the crime scene, I'll be in my room," Nate was speaking on the phone to his Chicago control supervisor.

"Give me a half hour," said Cliff. "I will tap on your door four times and hold up my badge."

"Okay, I'll wait for you," said Nate.

"What name are you going by?" asked Cliff.

"N. Sheldon."

"Sheldon, got it," said Cliff. "I'll be there as Field Officer Cliff Side."

Nate chuckled, "Cliff Side, I'll try and remember that."

"Don't strain yourself," said Cliff and clicked off.

No doubt the local cops would want Nate's identification and tell him to stay in his room for questioning. The hotel would be in lockdown for most of the night.

It was a bit difficult for the handsome six-foot-three Air Marshal to be a fly on the wall, but Nate hung back and tried to be invisible until they kicked him out of the lobby area. He watched the cops go about their business, securing the area. They were good.

Eventually the man who seemed to be in charge approached Nate and asked for his identification. "Are you a guest in the hotel, Mr. Sheldon?" he asked.

"Yes, I'm in room 406," Nate answered.

"Did you see this happen?"

"No but I heard gun-shots so I came out of my room."

The cop looked at him closely. "Weren't you afraid of being shot?"

"I guess that was a dumb thing to do, wasn't it?" Nate berated himself.

"What did you see?"

"Well, actually nothing. No one was in the hallway."

"You didn't see this happen?"

"Oh goodness, no. I only came down here after I heard all the sirens. Looked out the window and saw all the officers piling out of their cars. Figured it was safe at that point. Didn't hear any more shots."

"I see. Well, in that case, you need to stay in your room with the doors locked until someone comes to take your statement. The hotel is in lockdown until we find the perpetrator of this crime. Don't admit anyone into your room who is not in uniform. Understand?" He called over one of the cops who was just standing there and instructed her to take Mr. Sheldon to his room and make sure the room was secure.

A half hour later a quiet tap-tap-tap-tap came on the door. Nate walked up and peered through the peep hole. He saw a badge for three seconds and memorized the number. Nate disengaged three locks on the door, opening it slightly, quickly moved way back and hunkered down, gun drawn, the way he was trained to answer any door.

Slowly the door swung open. A man was crouched to one side, as he was trained to do.

"Your name and password," Nate asked softly.

"Field Officer Cliff Side, the password is nuts."

"Come in with your hands up," instructed Nate.

Cliff stepped in, laughing. "My God, man, it's you! What the hell you doin' in the Windy City?"

Nate laid his weapon down on the table. "I wish I knew," he laughed and stepped forward to envelope Cliff in a bear hug. He leaned back to look him in the face. "How long has it been–years?"

"A hundred years," said Cliff, pulling out a chair and laying his weapon on the table next to Nate's. "Are you involved in this mess downstairs?"

"Only that I called it in, so far as I know. But, there is other stuff we need to talk about."

"Okay shoot," said Cliff, "No, don't shoot!" he laughed.

Nate smiled, "You're just as crazy as ever. When are you going to grow up?"

"My wife says never," Cliff chuckled. "She thinks it's about time a man with six kids stopped acting like one."

"Six kids!" Nate exclaimed. "You've been busy."

"And you?" asked Cliff.

"Two, a boy and a girl."

"Slacker," said Cliff. "The Lord told you to populate the earth. What's holding you back?"

"I'm doing my part," Nate insisted. "Two by two, one of each kind."

"Well, buddy, we need to conduct some business here, before we can hit the bars and do the town."

"Yeah, I'm afraid there won't be any partying tonight."

"Too bad," said Cliff. "So, you called me. What's up?"

"You arrested a Mr. George F. George, arriving on United flight 302 earlier, right?"

"Yes, we did on the say-so of some idiot agent that only gave his badge number. Was that you?"

"Yes."

"We can only hold him so long. We had no idea what the hell was going on. Mr. George clammed up. You know about this?"

Nate nodded and walked over to the closet where he had stowed his luggage. He pulled his jacket off the hanger and brought it to the table. Using a clean towel from the bathroom, he spread it out on the table and carefully shook an item from the coat pocket. "I took this out of his pocket while he was arguing with the flight attendant. Haven't looked at it myself, but my prints are going to be on it. Maybe we can still retrieve his prints." Nate peered at a six-inch switch-blade. "Haven't looked at this, myself," said Nate.

"Oh-oh," said Cliff. "Hmm, in his pocket, you say?"

"Yup."

"On an airplane?"

"Yup, United Airlines' flight 302."

"But, how did he get this through security?" Cliff wondered.

"Same way I get my weapons through," said Nate. "It's not metal."

"No kidding?"

"The real question is, where did he get his hands on a weapon like this. You don't just order one on Ebay."

Nate looked closely at the weapon. "I'll be able to get a serial number off this. It's either American or Russian made."

"How can I get one of these?" asked Cliff.

"Not sure. Could be they are only issued to Air Marshalls, you know. The technology is top secret."

"So, how did the Russians get it?"

Nate gave Cliff a meaningful look. "Good question."

"You think Georgie-boy is a Russian spy?"

"Not really."

"Why do you say that?"

"Would the Russians be trying to ditch an American passenger plane into Lake Michigan?"

"Oh," said Cliff. "Well, if this new string of murders wasn't the doing of George, then who was it?"

"We don't know it had anything to do with George, do we?"

"Only that the perp got a cab driver, too."

"Oh no, what cab driver?"

"Yellow cab number 203-9642, waiting out at O'Hare, in the taxi lane. You know anything about it?"

"Well, I took a Yellow cab from the airport to here. But, I didn't take down his number. What time was it?"

"Tonight about an hour after United flight 302 came in. Found him with his throat slit, nice and neat."

"Dear Jesus." Nate held his head for a minute. Looking up he asked, "Any other clues?"

"Only the fifty-dollar bill and the Kentucky Fried Chicken wrappers in the front seat, covered in blood."

"Kentucky Fried? Oh no!"

"Hey, lots of people shop there. What's wrong with KFC anyway? It's one of my favorites."

"Nothing wrong, except that I had my cab stop at a KFC takeout window. What was he eating, do you know?"

"A chicken sandwich and medium coffee. Mean anything to you?"

Nate nodded, feeling sick.

"Funny thing was," Cliff continued, "the sales receipt was in the bag."

"Yeah?"

"It showed the chicken sandwich, coffee and a meal."

Nate turned white.

"There wasn't any meal," said Cliff. "We didn't know what to make of that, unless there was someone else in the cab at the time."

"It was me," Nate said, forlornly.

"You?"

"'Fraid so. And I took the meal with me. Look, here's the wrapper." Nate reached into his waste basket for the remains of his meal. "Only thing is, I didn't give the poor man a fifty-dollar bill."

"Ah … " said Cliff, thoughtfully. "Then it must have been a later fare. Someone was in there after you were."

"The murderer?" Nate mused.

"Could be. Yes, it must have been the murderer. The cabbie had not had time to put the money away."

"You have the bill, I hope," said Nate.

"Of course. What do you take us for, Sherlock?"

"How did you get it?"

"Oh wait. You're right. I'm sure the local cops have it."

"They bloody-well better have it."

"Wouldn't it be a shame if the murderer left behind his prints and DNA? Gotta love stupid criminals."

"I wish," said Nate. "More likely these folks are terrorists."

"Why do you say that?"

"The switchblade."

"But, we don't know that the murderer had any connection with George, do we?"

"Can't rule that out. Not if the same guy did the dirty business downstairs."

"You're right. Probably it's no coincidence. Well, pard, there is another curious thing about this George F. George fellow."

"How's that," asked Nate.

"It seems another passenger by the very same name took the Alaska Air/Virgin America flight out of D.C. for Dallas, around noon."

"Same guy?"

"How many George F. Georges do you know?"

"Now it makes sense—the unusual name I mean."

"Oh why?"

"The name is so silly. They wanted it to be memorable."

"So you think it was the same man?"

"Could have been. Doesn't matter really. It was either a distraction or a test."

Both men fell silent, deep in thought.

"Oh, I forgot something," said Nate. He got up and went to his closet again. He retrieved the small novel wrapped in a handkerchief, walked back and laid it on the table in front of Cliff. Gingerly he unwrapped the bundle, so as not to smear any possible prints. "Not sure I know what this means, but I took it out of the magazine pocket at seat 14B."

"Hmm," said Cliff, "Well, it's another piece of the puzzle. We'll book this as evidence. What's it about?"

Nate looked closely. "It appears to be written in Persian."

"Oh really? Now that is interesting," said Cliff. "Can you read it?"

"Only a very little bit," said Nate. "We'll have to send it to the lab for testing, first. You never know what all they can pick up from something like this. I mean he has handled it personally, had it on his person, in his house, his car, office, bathroom— anywhere he went. The lab can analyze everything that ever touched this book."

"Amazing."

"There might even be chemical residue picked up from surfaces where the book has laid. They can tell you what pages he read. In luck, they may even get his DNA, if he licked his fingers before he turned the pages."

"Wow," said Cliff. "Boy, I sure hope you used a clean handkerchief when you wrapped this thing."

"You betcha', My mother didn't raise no dummy," he laughed.

"Can you swear to that?"

~~~~~

Des Plaines PD

The suburban police department had done their job. By morning, every guest in the hotel had been interviewed and nearby streets and roads had been scoured. The evidence included the blood and fabric residue left on the fence at the swimming pool. Clearly the murderer had escaped over the fence, but he was bleeding, and so police tracking dogs were brought in to follow his trail. It led them to the spot where he had paused behind the building. Several drops of blood were there, where he evidently stood for some time.

The trail then went further away from the scene, continuing on behind buildings, until it crossed over to another street. He hid behind another building for a time, and then he came out to the curb and disappeared. The investigators reasoned that he had gotten into some kind of conveyance and left the area.

Records of all the local buses, taxicabs and Uber services would be examined to see if any fares were picked up at that exact spot. But, the murderer probably had an accomplice whom he called to pick him up. Cell phone records would show all the calls made from that area around that time and to whom.

There would be a lot of work involved in checking all those records and leads, but that was police work—a lot of drudgery and thousands of details to investigate a crime. Nevertheless, in the end, they would get their man.

~~~~~

Sea-Tac to YVR

Today was not going as well as Sally hoped. First the 8:05 AM plane was grounded for mechanical problems. Then she went on standby for the 9:40 AM flight, and missed that by just one—she was the first person cut off. The 12:04 PM flight was overbooked.

It was Sally's day off in Seattle. She had hoped to fly up to Vancouver today and see her mom. Of course, her only choice was to fly Alaska Airlines as an employee. Otherwise on another airline she would have to pay for a ticket. Unfortunately, her budget would not allow for that.

Sally checked her watch and studied the schedule again. She found a computer that wasn't busy at the moment and began searching. She tried various scenarios. This was going to require some creative scheduling. She couldn't afford to pay for a ticket. And so she searched every possible Alaska Airlines and Virgin America Airlines flights to see what she could do. Obviously, the closer the airport, the better, and so she tried Portland and then all the Los Angeles area flights. The problem with all of those was none flew directly to Vancouver. They all ended in Seattle, which meant that dozens of passengers from all those flights were changing planes in Seattle and crowding into flight 2242 from Seattle to Vancouver. No wonder that flight was full.

She was going to have to make at least one stop, maybe two or three. *Let's see*, she frowned and bit her lip. What was one of the busiest airports? How about Los Angeles? She could get into LAX. easily, but what does Alaska have out of LAX to

Vancouver? Nothing until after five. That wouldn't work. Maybe a smaller airport? She tried Boise, Portland, Sante Fe. No luck. Hey, wait a minute. Anchorage. Could she get out of here on a two o'clock flight and then turn around and fly back to Vancouver? That might work if she could drive out to the elder-care home, see her mom and get back in time to take the evening flight back to Seattle. No, on checking the schedule, it wouldn't work. The flights were too long and there were no connections that could get her back in one day. Too bad she had to work tomorrow.

There was only half an hour left before the next flight to Vancouver. Trying one last time for the 12:04 PM flight, suddenly one seat came open. Someone must have failed to check in. Quickly, Sally grabbed it and entered her ID. The good part was that she could make the reservation, no waiting on standby. Great! With a few more clicks, she had her seat on the flight and sent the boarding pass to the printer. Whew.

Sally walked over to the printer to grab her boarding pass, slipped it into her shoulder bag alongside her passport and new birth certificate.

The replacement birth certificate had arrived from the Portland County Clerk, just in time, before she had to leave for this assignment. Sally hadn't had time to study it, but she had seen enough to know that she had to confront her mother before Mom slipped into an even deeper state of dementia.

Sally was so upset about this. What was her mother thinking? This was craziness. Sally didn't know whether to be enraged, sad or simply confused. Whichever, she had to know who she was.

It was already 11:36 AM. Sally had to hustle to catch the 12:04 PM flight to Vancouver. She picked up her shoulder bag, placed the long strap crosswise over her chest and took off running. She had to go all the way from the end of Concourse A, through the terminal and out to the end of Concourse B. As much as possible she took the mechanical walkways, running down those like superwoman flying, dashing past old people pulling large suitcases and young women pushing baby carriages. Bummer. But, after that effort she was able to grab a ride on a Go-Buggy.

Totally out of breath and praying for help, she rushed toward the gate just as the "last call" announcement came over the speaker. "All passengers for Flight 2242 to Vancouver should be on board. The gate is closing." The uniformed employee was already turning off the machines and pulling the door closed. Sally ran up, chest heaving. "Hi," she said, opening her handbag. "I have a boarding pass right here." She pulled it out and waved it at the employee.

"Sorry ma'am, you have missed it," said the woman.

"Please try," begged Sally.

"I'll call them." She picked up the phone. "I have one more passenger," she said. "Have you closed yet?" As she waited, she reached for Sally's boarding pass and held it ready to run through the scanning machine. "Oh," she bit her lip. "Here," she said as she handed it back, "I'm so sorry. They have already buttoned up the cabin door and are starting to pull away."

Sally's shoulders slumped. Her face fell. "Darn."

"I'm really sorry," said the employee. She could see how disappointed Sally was. "Is there any other way I can help you?"

"No, the next Vancouver flight isn't until 5:40," said Sally. "Afraid that won't work for me. I need to get there sooner."

"Maybe there's another way—another airline?"

"Well …" Sally looked around. The counter was deserted now. "Maybe I can use your computer to look for another flight?"

"That's for employees, only. I'm sorry."

Sally reached for her employee ID and showed it to the women who took it in one hand. "Oh, yes, certainly. Go ahead and use it. Good luck. I hope things work out for you Ms. Millecan."

Sally moved over to the computer. If she could get to Vancouver by mid-afternoon she would still have time to drive over to the elder-care home and back in time to catch either the 7:20 or the 7:47 PM flight back to Seattle.

Sally started clicking on the keyboard. *Well, okay,* she thought, *I guess I'm going to have to break down and pay for a flight.* There were plenty of other airlines, but Sally had to try to use Alaska at least part of the way. If it wasn't so important to talk to her mother, she would have gone back to her hotel room hours ago.

Sally sighed and tried the Alaska flights to possibly connect with another airline. She knew of one possibility—Victoria. Oh yeah! Alaska Airline had a 1:47 PM to Victoria, British Columbia. Sally quickly looked up the airlines serving Victoria. What kind of flight could she get out of there and how much would it cost? Would it break her budget? Ah yes, Air Canada had several. *Let's see, if I hop on the 1:47, I'll arrive in Victoria at 2:34 PM. Bingo! Air Canada Express-Jazz has a flight #8070 leaving at 3:20. Perfect! How much? $169.58, plus another $35 for the rental car. I can do this.*

She would arrive in Vancouver at 3:47 PM—plenty of time.

Seated by a window, Sally gazed for a while at the spectacular scenery. In no time they were out over Puget Sound heading north toward Victoria. She had been so busy trying to arrange and catch this flight that she had no time to think about her replacement birth certificate. But now the turbulence of questions crashed into her thoughts like a tsunami. She had to clear her mind for a few minutes of much-needed rest. What were some of the methods and tricks she had learned in her yoga class?

First she leaned her head back, closed her eyes and inhaled a long slow breath, counting to six. Without tightening up, she held for two counts, letting it out, slowly counting backward six, five, four, three, two, one, and then relaxing for a count of six. She repeated this exercise three times. As she relaxed, she imagined the tension washing down over her and out through her toes into the floor. And then she pictured herself in a peaceful place, beside a clear gentle stream. She saw the water bubbling over pebbles. A lazy brown trout hung in the stream, facing into the flow, its fins moving slowly, just enough to hold it in place. Its gills pumped the life-giving water through and over the pink oxygen-absorbing membranes. From time to time Sally repeated the relaxing breaths again, and fell asleep.

Twenty minutes later she awakened to the pleasant humming of the airplane gliding smoothly over the ocean, preparing to line up for Victoria, situated on the southern end of Vancouver Island. Sunlight gleamed off snow-capped mountains in the distance, remote and incredibly beautiful. This was one of the world's most spectacular landings, approaching over the water.

She had to concentrate on this experience and not let her personal concerns intrude. There would be plenty of time for that.

On the ground in Victoria, she had no more than a forty-five-minute turnaround before she boarded the flight to Vancouver. This terminal was not nearly as vast as Seattle's. Fortunately she could stay right here in this concourse, without having to go through security again. First a quick rest room trip to refresh herself, and then she looked over the offerings in the food booths. She needed something more than junk food and so she chose a full meal and sat down at a table to eat.

Finishing her food, she stopped at the sundries shop and picked up a slim book to read—one she could slip into her purse. She hoped it would fill her mind for a while. In choosing a book she bypassed the best sellers and political alarmists and went directly to the Westerns. She selected one with a buff-looking cowboy in a Stetson hat, on the cover. This should do it.

Chapter 9 Holed Up

Kabandha Patches up J. M.

Kabandha grabbed a first aid kit from their meager supplies. "Mohammad! Come here," the giant woman commanded.

He froze in the doorway, afraid to move.

"Come here, you idiot!" She indicated a straight-backed chair.

He sheepishly moved forward.

"Your orders were not to call me," she accused. "But, you're here now. I'll have to patch you up."

"Thank you," he simpered, speaking in Farsi.

She slapped him with a well-muscled arm. "Speak in English, you fool!" She hissed as she began cutting away the bloody garment. "You'll give us away."

J. Mohammad-Mutawassit flinched. He guiltily realized he frequently spoke Farsi to the attractive woman across the hall.

As she worked, cleaning up his wound, Kabandha continued the questioning. "What happened here?"

"My hand was cut on the fence."

"What fence?"

"I did not know the swimming pool was fenced in."

"What were you doing at a swimming pool? Those were not your orders."

"I had to escape the police."

"You called the police?"

"No, someone called the police." Mohammad winced as she roughly applied disinfectant to the wound and rubbed vigorously. "Ouch, watch it!"

"Coward!" She sneered as she wrapped his hand and continued cutting away the garment. "How did you get all this blood from that little tiny scratch?"

"Some of it was from the bodies, I suppose."

"Bodies! What in the name of Allah did you do?"

"It was necessary."

"How many bodies?"

"Three of them," he bragged, "all infidels. Allah be praised."

"You fool!" The ugly woman backed into a fighting stance. Suddenly, a switchblade gleamed in her hand. "You have compromised our operation!"

"No, no," he fell to his knees. "Mercy," he begged. He knew the punishment for such an offense would be swift.

Kabandha stood over him with an evil glare, the knife raised in her muscled striking arm.

Moments passed. Mohammad quivered and soiled his trousers.

"A life for a life," the horrid woman screamed and plunged the knife into his flesh. Mohammad fainted.

It was only a flesh wound and would heal if she decided to care for him. She stood over him watching as the blood flowed onto the bare floor. In minutes he could be dead.

A change of plans was already formulating in her clever mind. Did she need this bumbling fool to fulfill her mission? Or could she continue with the fewer number of men remaining in her cell? Already the one known as George was compromised. Perhaps she could send Mohammad, now wanted for murder, to deal with that numbskull George. Both of them had failed. Yes, she could use Mohammad for that purpose. He would not survive long in this city, anyway.

Her mind was made up, she could still use him. So she moved into the tiny kitchen for towels to bind his wound and save his miserable life. More rags would mop up the mess.

~~~~~

Sunday School Class

Volunteer teacher Sharon McGillicuddy opened the lesson plan for the day and gazed around the table at her small group of young teenagers. These were the kids that she hoped to reach before they got into trouble. There was so much evil lurking out there, ready to recruit them into a drugged-out dream-world. Sharon knew first-hand what could happen. She dealt with it every day on the job.

Of course, these were the privileged kids with at least one parent or guardian who brought them to Sunday school. But, evil was no respecter of class. The opioid epidemic was claiming lives every day. Social media was luring kids into trouble. Marijuana had been made legal, as if it was harmless, but Sharon knew otherwise. If a young person managed to avoid those traps there was alcohol and nicotine beckoning, plus the overpowering assault of sexual hormones was just around the corner, ready to lead them into STD's and/or early parenthood. Dear God, what could she do?

For the moment, Sharon, set the lesson plan aside, and addressed the group. "Hi, Everybody, and welcome back. Is anyone new here today? You don't have to raise your hand, just nod or wink at me." Sharon smiled at each one, in turn. "For those of you who don't know me, my name is Sharon, but you should know this: in my day job, I am Officer McGillicuddy," she said making a fake gun sign with one hand.

Everyone looked at her with new eyes.

"Yeah, I'm a cop," she admitted, "but, don't worry, I'm not here to arrest anybody."

"Whew, that's a relief," said Danny, the class clown.

"Something I should know?" kidded Sharon.

He laughed, "Ha-ha, I'm not telling." He crossed his arms and sat back. The others laughed.

"She'll get you, if you don't watch out," squeaked Charlie. He was only twelve, Danny's younger brother. His voice had not changed yet.

Laughter relieved the tension.

"In case you clowns have any doubts about me, I'm here because I get sick of associating with all those criminals I have to haul into the hoosegow during my day job. Today's my day off and a chance to be with some really good kids. That's you, you and you," she smiled and pointed around the group one at a time.

"And I assume you are here for somewhat the same reason, right?" Sharon asked.

"Naw, my mom makes me," said one. The others laughed.

"Good for her," said Sharon. "Now, you all studied the lesson for the day, of course," she said, looking around at everyone burying their heads in the lesson book as if they could absorb it in a few seconds. "Never mind," she laughed. "Neither did I." Ten pairs of eyes looked up in astonishment. "Ha! Gotcha'!" she said and chuckled. "Okay, let's get started. Would someone please volunteer to read the scripture for today?"

"Seeing no one, I'll read it," she sighed. "Please open your Bibles to …"

~~~~~

Coffee Hour

After taking time to put her room to rights and stack the chairs, Sharon was a bit late arriving at the coffee hour between church school and worship. She chose a black coffee and searched for the cookies. A small hand reached up over the table and grabbed the last one off the plate. Sharon grinned at the tiny girl dressed in a frilly pink dress, white tights and white patent leather shoes. The pudgy little hand smashed the cookie part-way into the rosebud mouth. Cookie crumbs covered the sweet face.

A harried mother walked up and took the little girl's free arm, pulling her away from the table. "I'm sorry," she apologized. "This little sneak has already had her share."

"No problem at all," said Sharon. "I don't need a cookie, believe me."

"None of us do," said the mother laughing. "But, you deserve it, my dear, considering how hard you work."

"Who me—not!" laughed Sharon.

"On the contrary, I see what you do with the kids," said the mother. "My boys are in your class."

"Oh?"

"Danny and Charlie," she said laughing, "the terrible two."

"Oh, yeah," Sharon nodded. "Those two boys are my absolute favorites. They are great! You must be proud of them."

"That is nice of you to say. But, no doubt they give you a hard time."

"Not at all. They are wonderful boys. You just keep doing what you're doing."

"Well, thank you, Officer McGillicuddy. I appreciate that."

"Ah, so they told you," Sharon raised her eyebrows. "Yes, it's true, I'm a cop."

"That's a good thing. We thank you for your service. And then, on top of what you do all week, you come out here on Sunday morning. That goes above and beyond."

"Thank you."

"Well, I've got to get this little dickens into the nursery. Excuse me." The woman smiled, took the little girl by the hand and headed down the hall.

"Can I refill your coffee, Sharon?" asked a man's voice behind her.

Sharon turned and almost bumped into the tall good-looking man speaking to her.

"Oh hi," she said. "I didn't know you attended here. You're … uh …" She searched for a name.

"Rob … Rob Goodrich, at your service. Remember me, the rotten egg king?"

Sharon laughed. "Of course, I remember you, Rob. How could I forget? It just took me a second to think of your name."

"Remember it this way," he said. "If I wasn't so good and rich, I would have to rob."

"Got it. Robbers are good and rich." She giggled. "Do you attend here often, Rob?"

He bowed his head, "Not as often as I'd like, but now that I know who else comes here, I'll be here every Sunday."

"Now, now, Mr. Goodrich, you know that is not a good reason to attend worship." She sipped on her coffee.

"Whatever works, don't you think?"

"You've got me there."

"In fact, I've been away at school, so this was my first opportunity."

"Oh, where do you attend?"

"I'm at State U." Just then the lights blinked twice. "I think it is time to go in. May I take your arm?"

"My hand, maybe," she smiled, placed her cup on the table, and offered her hand.

Rob felt like kissing it, and maybe her lips, too.

~~~~~

Vancouver Confrontation

Sally folded the Western novel and slid it into her bag, stowing the bag under the seat in front of her. Securely buckled in, she watched out the window as the ground rose toward the airplane.

Air Canada Express-Jazz flight number eighty-seventy's wheels kissed the tarmac in Vancouver BC, with only the merest peep of sound. The pilot expertly guided the vessel onto the taxiway precisely on time. It cautiously glided up to the gate like a gigantic cruise ship docking in Miami.

Sally hoped her mom would be having one of her good days. For some reason, she felt nervous and jittery. This had to work. She had to know the truth.

.

Seated in her wheel chair, Ferrell Millecan looked up when Sally entered the room. This was a good sign.

"Hello, Mother," said Sally.

"Hello," said Ferrell. "Happy birthday."

"You remembered!" Sally brightened, suddenly feeling optimistic. This just might be her day.

Ferrell merely smiled and held out her hand. At a loss for words, Sally took it and leaned down to kiss her mother on the cheek. She pulled up a side chair, sat by her mother's side and blinked away tears that threatened to fall.

"I'm glad you are home safely," said Ferrell. "How was school today?"

"Um ... school?"

"Did those boys chase you home again? You didn't see any strange men hanging around, did you?"

Sinking back, Sally realized her mother thought they were back in their old neighborhood in Vancouver. She had to go along. "The boys weren't so bad today, Mom," she said. "And did you have a good day, too?"

"I worked, same as usual." Ferrell shrugged.

"Uh-huh," said Sally. "Well, thank you for that, Mom."

"I do what I have to do. No big deal."

"It is to me, Mom. Otherwise, I wouldn't have this home and be able to walk to school."

"I suppose you are right. I never thought of it that way."

"Can I get you anything, Mom?"

"No, thank you. It's your birthday. I'll make supper. Maybe we can go out for a treat. I wish I had a birthday present for you." She sighed. "Maybe next year we can afford a trip."

"That's okay, Mom. You do your best."

"Yes, I do. I really try hard."

"I know that, and I love you for it," said Sally, wondering how she could steer her mother into telling her the truth. "There is one thing you can do for my birthday, Mom, and it won't cost you any money."

"How's that?"

"This would mean more to me than the finest birthday party," said Sally.

"Okay, what is it?" Ferrell asked warily.

Sally took her hand, "I want you to tell me about when I was born. What was it like?"

"Oh, I can't do that." Ferrell shook her head.

"Why not? I'm old enough, Mom. I know about babies."

Ferrell clenched her teeth and looked away.

"Was it so bad?" asked Sally. "I mean was it painful or anything. Did you scream and cry like in the movies?"

Ferrell turned back, a faraway look in her eyes. "You were so beautiful."

"Beautiful? Really? I thought newborn babies were ugly."

"Oh no, you were the most beautiful thing I had ever laid my eyes on. I was supposed to give you up, but when that nurse put your little body on my chest and covered us with a soft baby blanket, you just snuggled right down as if you were a part of me."

Sally gulped. *What did this mean? Was I illegitimate? Didn't she even know my father? Had she planned to put me up for adoption?* "And so, you couldn't give me up, right?"

"I knew I had to keep you. I loved you."

"Mother's love is strong, they say," Sally managed. "What's it like?"

Ferrell's mind went back. "It's like this huge enormous love, something that just fills you up and bursts all around you. You almost grow bigger. It is more wonderful than anything you ever experienced." She paused, remembering. "It's like, now, for the first time in your life, you know why you were put on earth. It all makes sense."

"What makes sense? I don't understand."

"Life. Life makes sense."

"Is it just a feeling," asked Sally, "or is it a physical thing, too?"

"Oh it is all of that together. When that baby puts her little mouth up to your breast and sucks, your whole chest tingles and swells. You feel your milk come in. It is something like an orgasm, only better, sweeter, closer."

Ferrell's face had become serene with a little smile. Her eyes were half closed. "Now it all makes sense," she breathed. "It's the culmination of the sex act."

Sally gave her mother's hand a little squeeze. "That's wonderful, Mother. Tell me the rest."

Ferrell's face seemed to jerk into a different place, "What rest? I get rest—too much rest. I hate rest."

"Not that rest. I mean the rest of the story. Tell me the rest of the story about my birth. You know, the people around you, the doctors, nurses, visitors. They must have loved the baby, too." Sally hoped to find out who came to see her. Maybe it was her father.

Ferrell's face clouded. "Visitors ... bah!" She almost spat. "It was goo-goo this, and ga-ga that. I despised them."

"Despised who? How could you hate them? Didn't they love the baby too?"

Ferrell looked away. "They wanted to take my baby."

"You must be mistaken, Mother."

"But, I fooled them. I took my baby. She would never be theirs. I took her home. I named her Sally Miller. They would never find me." She laughed, "Ha-ha, that evil man tried to get you away, but I hid. I ran and hid."

"Where, Mother? Where did we hide?"

"Why, right here, Sally, here in Vancouver. Don't you know where we are?"

"Yes, Mom, we're right here in Vancouver. But, we have moved so many times, I forget. Thank you for reminding me."

"Right here in Vancouver," Ferrell repeated as if to assure herself.

"Mommy, next year for my birthday, can we please take a trip?" Sally pretended to be Ferrell's young daughter.

"Maybe, we'll see."

"I'd like to go back to the place where I was born, back to Portland, Oregon."

"No, no, never back there." Ferrell shook her head vigorously. "Not Portland."

"Is Oregon dangerous, Mommy?"

"Very dangerous. We can never go back."

"Would the bad man come after me?"

Ferrell nodded her head, "He would never quit. That awful man tried to take you away. He chased us."

"Okay, Mommy, we don't have to go there. I'm sorry I asked." Sally patted her hand to calm her down.

Ferrell sighed, and half-smiled at Sally.

Sally took a chance, "I understand, now, why you had to change my name from Miller to Millecan. That was to keep me safe, wasn't it?"

Ferrell nodded.

"You had to keep me safe from the man who wanted to take me, didn't you?"

"He would have come. He would have found us."

"You named me Sally Miller. What was my name going to be if you hadn't kept me?"

Ferrell tried to curl up in a fetal position. "I don't … Noooo," she cried, shaking her head wildly.

Sally rubbed her mother's arm, "But, once we were over into Canada, we were safe. You took care of us. We were mostly safe."

Ferrell relaxed a bit.

Sally continued, "But, you had to always be careful, to make sure he didn't find us. That is why you had to change our name again, and we had to move—so he would never find us. You did the right thing."

"He never found us," said Ferrell, calmer now. "Never found us … He'll never find us. I'll keep you safe."

Sally waited

All at once, Ferrell clenched her hands and pursed her lips. She shook her head slightly and looked away. Transformed, her face clouded over. She glared back at Sally as if she was a stranger. "Who are you? Get away from me." She pushed on Sally. "Leave me alone with my baby. Go away!"

Sally stood and started to back away.

"Get out, you thief!" Ferrell shouted.

"Mother, it's me, Sally, your daughter."

Ferrell started screaming, "Help! Help me!" A nurse rushed into the room. She took hold of Ferrell's arm. "Shh, you're okay. Quiet down, Ferrell. You're safe now." Ferrell broke into sobs. Sally looked on in horror.

The nurse motioned for Sally to leave the room. "She'll be all right in a few minutes. She has these episodes sometimes. She believes someone is here to steal her baby," the nurse said sadly. "Perhaps you should go, now."

Sally paused. She brushed away a tear. "Goodbye, Mother," she said softly. "Happy birthday." She picked up her bag and tiptoed out.

Chapter 10 Chicago

Lab Report

*N*ate would be staying over in Chicago for a day or two, maybe longer. He hated to be away from home this long, missing out on the visit with Rob who would be leaving for Italy soon. But, that made it less lonely for Nan, now that she had both kids home. Nate was happy that Rob was taking an interest in watching over his sister. The next couple of years in Joy's life would be perilous in terms of male relationships, while she was learning the ropes. She needed her dad, even though she was fighting for her independence at the same time. *Is that what was meant by the phrase "Sixteen, going on thirty?"* Nate grinned to himself.

Oh well, it was time to get up and get going.

Nate went through his morning shave, shower and dressing for the day with his usual efficiency. He had to go in to headquarters this morning to meet with Cliff Side. That wasn't his name. Darn it! Nate had been trying to think of Cliff's real last name for hours. It had been looping around in his brain just out of reach.

The local cops had done a great job of processing the two crime scenes, lifting prints and DNA and cataloging hundreds of clues. Already they had matched the two murders as having been committed by the same person. The third victim, the manager, was still in intensive care. Cliff and Nate hoped to interview him today.

So far, the police had been unable to find the murder suspect, nor did they have any theory as to motive. This was where the feds came in. Nate and Cliff had a theory of motive, which they had not shared with the police.

~~~~~

Cliff and Nate

"Come in," said Cliff. "Grab a seat. I see you got your coffee. Good."

"Good morning," said Nate. He pulled out a chair from a conference table and sat down.

Cliff gestured at the papers spread out on the table. "We've got the lab reports back on the novel and the switchblade." He handed Nate a one-page printout. "It runs to several pages, but this is a condensed version. Take a gander."

Nate picked up the paper and began reading. "Mmm," he muttered from time to time, nodding his head occasionally. At length he looked up. "Well, what do you know? Seems our little Georgie-Porgie has been a busy boy."

"Yeah," said Cliff, "fooling around with chemical agents and bomb making materials."

"Somehow, I don't think he was planning on taking down that airliner with a six-inch switchblade," said Nate.

"So, maybe this was just another trial run."

"Testing to see just how much he could get away with."

"There's the motive."

"Motive for that trip, but it doesn't explain the murders." Nate thought for a moment. "Try this on for size," he said. "Suppose Georgie had an accomplice?"

"No doubt he did and still does, more than one."

"I mean an accomplice on the plane."

"Possible," Cliff agreed.

"This accomplice saw me, more or less, pat George down for weapons and then lift the knife out of his pocket."

"Seeing this, his conclusion would be?"

"Bingo. Federal Air Marshal."

Cliff snapped his fingers and pointed at Nate. "Way to go, Sherlock. And then, guess what happens when he walks off the plane. He sees us pick up George and hustle him off."

"He puts two and two together and realizes I put the finger on George."

"He must have waited around until you got off the plane," said Cliff.

"And I thought I was so clever, changing my disguise. The change of shirt, shoes, gloves and the new beard didn't fool him at all."

"He was watching you, Nate. That's why."

"Boy, was I dumb," Nate moaned and shook his head.

"Not at all, friend, you were very smart."

"He was even smarter."

"Not true. They all make mistakes. Just remember, Nate, he didn't get you, did he? Good grief, look at the trail he left behind when he committed those murders. His goose is cooked. We'll get this guy."

"Thanks. But, why didn't he find me at the hotel?"

"What name did you use when you checked in?"

"I normally use a different name and ID, altogether."

"See? I told you. You were smarter."

"Thank you, Mother," said Nate, grinning and rolling his eyes.

"Don't forget to thank your father, too," Cliff chuckled.

"And all my teachers, grandparents, aunts, uncles, pastors, scout leaders, mentors and friends," he said, lightly punching Cliff on the arm.

"So, what do you think? Do we have enough to hold him?"

"George?"

"Yeah."

"Boy, I don't know. What's the penalty for carrying a dangerous weapon onto a plane?"

"Not enough," said Cliff. "It's a civil offense to carry a gun into an airport, punishable by a fine of up to $10,000, but the authorities base it on a number of factors, including the type of weapon, the intent, whether the person resisted arrest, and whether it is a first offense.

"Some states are even writing new laws to deal with terrorism. For instance, in Texas it is illegal to threaten terrorism, which is defined by several terms. Even so, it is only a misdemeanor punishable by up to $4,000 fine and 180 days in jail, maximum."

"Interesting," said Nate, "and so, we can only hold him for twenty-four hours, right?"

"Well, that depends," said Cliff. "The police can hold you for up to 24 hours before they must charge you with a crime or release you. They can apply to hold you for up to 36 or 96 hours if you're suspected of a serious crime like murder. You can be held without charge for up to fourteen days if you're arrested under the Terrorism Act."

"Man, you are just a font of information," said Nate. "So, we have to let George go or apply the Patriot Act. There are tons of rules in that, too."

"Right, but remember this truism: Show me a rule, and I'll show you a loophole."

"Ha-ha, well that is one definition I ought to know by heart." Nate continued in a sing-song voice, "An act of domestic terrorism is any act with the intent and for the purpose of supporting, planning, conducting, or concealing an act of domestic or international terrorism against the United States, citizens or residents of the United States or their property."

"Tah-Dah! You've got that one down pat. Looks like we are covered," said Cliff. "What say we grab our jackets and head up to the hospital? I'd like to have a word with Mr. Alan Bartle."

"Sounds like a plan." Nate agreed, as he stood up, grabbed his jacket and straightened his necktie.

~~~~~

Alan Bartle Interview

"I assume you know where we're going," said Nate, not wanting to appear less than trusting of his friend's directional abilities.

"Uh, yeah," said Cliff as he guided the car onto the expressway. "I think I know the way to Presence."

"Presence?" Nate queried. "Do you mean Heaven?"

"Yeah, sometimes it's the last step before Heaven." Cliff laughed. "However, in this case Presence Resurrection Medical Center is the primary receiving hospital for O'Hare Airport and vicinity. They claim to treat over forty thousand patients a year."

"Wow, that's a whole lot of air-sickness."

Cliff laughed, "Well, no, they also serve the neighboring communities of Park Ridge and Des Plaines. It's a complete hospital with every kind of service, from heart to orthopedic, sports medicine, dialysis, you name it."

"I see."

"Look, if you want to do me a favor you can program the address into the GPS on the dash, or into your phone. Just in case you get lost, understand? I won't need it."

"Okay, go ahead."

"It's 7435 West Talcott Avenue, Chicago, Illinois."

"Hold it, not so fast. Seven, four, three, what?" asked Nate, punching in numbers.

"Five," said Cliff.

"Go ahead."

"West … Talcott. That's T-A-L-C-O-T-T, Avenue."

"Got it. Thanks."

The Holiday Inn manager was out of intensive care. This was good. He had been moved to a private room on a private floor. This arrangement was an extra security measure used in cases where the patient needed protection and was standard in the case of gunshot wounds. All visitors were carefully screened.

Cliff and Nate stepped up to the security guard and presented their IDs.

"Yessirs, you can go on in," the guard checked their IDs and waved them forward. "Mr. Bartle is down this hall to your left. Room 431. There is no name on the door."

"No name?"

"Just another security precaution, sir. Here are your IDs, but hold onto them. You will need them one more time."

Bartle was sitting up in bed, watching a game on TV. A uniformed policewoman sat in the only chair. When Cliff knocked gently, she arose and walked over. "Hello, sir," she greeted Cliff first. "Please come in, one at a time. May I please see your ID?" she asked. Carefully checking the name and comparing the picture with Cliff's face, she asked, "And what is your purpose in visiting this room?"

"We are here to question the witness in a crime."

"The witness's name, please."

"Alan Bartle."

She waved Cliff in and turned to Nate. "Your name and ID, please, sir."

"Nate Sheldon, and I'm here to question Mr. Bartle, as well."

Again she scrutinized the ID and compared the picture with Nate's face. "You're okay," she waved him in and took her place, leaning against the wall and watching them. She spoke their names and purpose into a communicator.

"Mr. Bartle?" asked Cliff.

"Yeah, and you are?"

"My name is Cliff. Cliff Side. And this is Agent Nate Sheldon with Homeland Security." He gestured toward Nate, in both cases giving their false last names.

"Hello," said Nate. Bartle merely nodded.

"We are investigating the murder and assault that took place at the Holiday Inn Express in Des Plaines, Illinois. We understand that you were seriously injured. Is that correct?"

"Yes,"

"I know you have been interviewed already, but would you mind telling us what happened, in your own words?"

"Well," he began, "as I told the cops, I was working as the manager that night, back in my office, when the alarm went off."

"What alarm is that, sir?"

"Well, the front desk is equipped with a call button, if they need help."

"I see. Go on, please."

"And so, I immediately got up from my desk and went to see what was wrong. As I came down the hall I heard loud voices from the front desk. Some man was trying to get something. He had come around and pushed Rosie, our receptionist, down on the floor. I heard her screaming. When I heard that I started running. This strange man was trying to work the computer. I tapped 911 and he shot me. Rosie tried to escape and he shot her, too." Bartle paused for breath and gazed forlornly out the window, a sad look on his face.

"You are doing fine," said Cliff. "Please continue when you are ready."

"Well, I heard the man put down the gun and try to work the computer. But, then the police sirens started, and he ran.

"When they got there, I was treated by the emergency crew and taken to this hospital where they took great care of me. They saved my life and I am very grateful. It was only later when I learned that Rosie had died, God rest her soul. Have you caught the guy, officer?"

"Not yet, but we will."

"Why did he kill that poor woman?" Bartle moaned. "What was he doing? Was he trying to rob us?"

Cliff ignored Bartle's questions. "You said when you first ran down the hall you heard voices. Could you understand any of the words?"

Bartle shook his head, "No not really. They didn't make any sense."

"That's okay. Just tell us if you heard anything, any random words."

Bartle thought for a minute. "I think the man said something like 'try them all'. Not sure about that, and then she said 'Mavis, Davis, Avis,' and … " He shook his head.

Cliff waited.

Nate said, "You thought you heard Mavis, Davis, Avis. That's very good. Think hard, were there any more similar words, any more like those?"

Bartle pursed his lips and frowned. "Umm, well, she named some more words that sort of rhymed. It was crazy, so I probably heard her wrong."

"Just try, please," said Nate. "Anything."

"Well, could it have been Travis, Mattis, Marvis…words like that? Why would she say that? Makes no sense."

"Anything you heard will help us," Cliff encouraged the man.

"Well, I know what I said."

"Good, what did you say?"

"I yelled at him, 'What is the meaning of this? What are you doing?' "

"Very good, sir. And so you must have had a reason to ask those questions. What was the man doing that caused your reaction?"

"He had come around the counter and was operating the computer."

"And then he shot you, right?"

"That's right."

Everyone was quiet for a minute, each one thinking.

Bartle spoke first. "I just thought of something else the man said."

"Excellent," said Cliff.

"He said to her, 'Give me your damned register' she said something about 'everything is on the computer these days'.

"You see, we don't keep paper records anymore. I think that is when he shoved her down. I didn't see that, but I heard her crash and start screaming."

"I have a question," said Nate. Everyone looked at him. "After he shot the two of you, did he continue working at the computer?"

"Yes, I could hear him. I couldn't see, but I heard him."

"Can you take a guess at how long he stayed working at the computer before he ran?" asked Nate.

"Hard to say. It seemed like forever before the police got there."

"Was he there more than one minute?"

"Oh yeah, maybe two or three."

"Could it have been five minutes."

"Possibly."

"Six, seven, eight?"

"No more than ten minutes."

"So he operated the computer between three and ten minutes, would you say?"

"Yeah, at the outside. But, I was bleeding and in terrible pain. Maybe I passed out for a while. I don't remember." Bartle moved off the pillows and laid his head down.

Seeing that Mr. Bartle seemed to be tiring, Cliff said, "Thank you, Mr. Bartle. You have been very helpful. We'll let you rest now."

"You are going to get that guy, aren't you?" Bartle pleaded.

"We'll give it our very best, I promise," said Nate. "If you think of anything more, we'll probably stop back in a day or two. In the meantime, please get well, okay?"

"I will," said Bartle, "Thanks for coming."

Back in the car, Cliff asked, "Well, what do you think?"

"The murderer was trying to find my room number," said Nate.

"You think?"

"No question about it, Cliff. On the airplane I checked in as N. Mavis. But, at the Inn I was N. Sheldon."

"Yup, no question. Smart thing you did, changing your name."

"I suppose so, but that poor woman didn't deserve to die in my place, did she?"

~~~~~

Lobbyist Directive Pooh-poohed

Back at the office Cliff and Nate worked hard, bringing all their notes up to date and thinking about the case. "We can question George for a few more days, maybe," said Cliff. "but, we'll have to let him go without bringing charges. It's more important to round up the entire cell."

"Yeah, you're right."

As Cliff sorted through fresh directives in from Washington that morning, he came across one thing of interest. "Listen to this, Nate. Home office is warning about possible lobbyist connections."

"Oh, how's that?"

Cliff paused while reading, holding up one finger. "Um ... one second."

Nate watched and waited.

"I guess it is an unsubstantiated rumor. Something to the effect that they suspect some lobbyist is working for a terrorist group ... It's not real clear. Umm ... they are trying to bring down an American passenger liner."

"Well, so what else is new?"

"Nothing much, except ..." Cliff was still reading the directive.

"I guess some doh-doh thinks that they are putting spies into airplane manufacturer's boards of directors, officers and engineering departments and trying to somehow plant something into brand new passenger planes."

"Brilliant," said Nate. "And how much is this desk-jockey getting paid for coming up with these hare-brained ideas?

Besides, how could spies be on passenger planes, anyway? No way can they be pilots. We've been there, done that."

"Not pilots. They say it could be through other means. All sorts of people service the planes, you know—mechanics, food service people, luggage handlers. Who else?"

"Yeah, but none of these people actually stay on the plane, do they?"

"How about the cleaning people?"

"Hmm, I suppose," mused Nate. "but cleaning people do their thing and leave, and then, their work is inspected."

"Could something be planted in luggage and then, just shipped off?"

"Well, I suppose it is possible, but no luggage is allowed without an accompanying passenger. Besides, all luggage goes through more than one inspection. The terrorists have not been able to make it work in over sixteen years."

"Flight attendants?" asked Cliff.

"Not likely," Nate replied. "They have to pass rigorous background checks, and annual exams."

"Oh," Cliff put the paper aside, adding it to the pile.

~~~~~

The George Problem

"Dammit, Kabandha, how long are we going to stay holed up in this place? I'm going stir-crazy."

"Shut your yap, Mohammad. You want stir-crazy? Just step out onto the street and you'll spend the rest of your miserable life in a cell."

A disgruntled J. Mohammad Mutawassit picked up a well-thumbed magazine and plopped down on an old sofa. The springs sagged with his weight.

"Come out here and help," said Kabandha.

Mohammad heaved his large belly off the sofa and shuffled out to the tiny kitchen table.

"Sit your lazy butt down," she ordered. "We need to decide what we are going to do."

Mohammad adjusted his extra-large sized butt cheeks onto the small chair and leaned his elbows on the table.

"All right, I'm listening. What are our choices?" asked Mohammad.

"Well, only two as I see it. We can let them squeeze George, or we can take care of the problem."

"I don't see how we get to George. He's on ice."

"Maybe a lawyer can spring him."

"Yeah, sure, on the grounds that he is such a nice innocent bystander, minding his own business, unjustly arrested, etcetera."

"Grounds aren't important."

"Huh?"

"It's all up to the judge."

Mohammad merely stared at her.

"You have to have the right judge."

"You got a judge?" he asked.

"Maybe," she said slyly.

"Will wonders never cease?" said Mohammad. "I'm impressed."

"Let's just say, our people are everywhere."

"Okay, so someone springs George and then what?"

"And then you take care of George."

"Eliminate the problem, so to speak?"

"Right."

"I can handle that."

~~~~~

Sari, the Snitch

At that very moment, the woman who lived across the hall was watching the evening news, pencil and paper in hand. She was waiting for the news report about that poor lady who was murdered at the Holiday Inn. She had already seen the report several times, and so was poised to write down a phone number. Citizens were told to be on the lookout for a man following the description, who was wanted in connection with two senseless murders of a woman and a cab driver. The segment always ended with an appeal for help from citizens, along with a number to call.

Sari had made up her mind. She was going to make the call. This lawlessness and mass murder had gone on long enough. It was time for Americans of all faiths to put a stop to it. Sari was a good Muslim, peace-loving, moderate and conservative, and she had seen enough. It was time for the silent majority of honest law-abiding and patriotic people of faith to stop the madness.

And so, Sari picked up the phone.

A recorded message announced, "You have reached the Des Plaines Police Department Anonymous Tip-Line. Your message is being recorded. You may leave your message after the tone."

Sari cleared her throat and began, "Hello, I'm calling about the murders. I have no proof, but people in our apartment building have been talking about the couple that live in apartment 2B. We just think they have been acting strange. We know they have weapons and we've heard yelling. Also there were some bloody clothes and rags in the dumpster. Maybe you could check them out, just in case, okay?

"I won't leave my name. The apartment address is ..." Her voice shaking, Sari left the street address and quickly hung up.

Chapter 11 Rob

Gets Phone Number

*A*fter the worship service Rob had picked up a church directory. He hoped to find Sharon's number and see what he could do. He thumbed through the M's. Ah–McGillicuddy–bingo! But, it didn't list Sharon, only Terry and Rose McGillicuddy. Hmm, well, he would just have to put on his most charming voice and give it a try. He ran his left finger over the listing while he held his cell phone in his right hand and tapped in the number with his right thumb.

"You must dial a one or a zero before dialing this number," said a recorded voice.

Rob tried again. A distant phone rang ten times and then went to voice mail. Rob clicked off. This time he scrutinized the number shown on his display and compared it with the church phone directory. *Oh darn, I missed one number. Fat fingers.* He erased his error and typed in the right number. It started ringing.

"McGillicuddy residence," answered a cheerful feminine voice.

"Hello, Mrs. McGillicuddy, this is Rob Goodrich. We may have met at church."

"I don't remember Rob, sorry. I've met Nate and Nan and their daughter Joy, several times. Nice people."

"That's my family," said Rob. "I've been away at school. Did you see me on Sunday?"

"Hmm, sorry Rob."

"I was sitting with Sharon."

"Oh, now I know you. I noticed Sharon sitting with a stranger. Holding hands, actually," she laughed. "Well, I guess you weren't strange to her, huh?"

"That was me, Mrs. McGillicuddy. I'm calling to talk with Sharon. Is she there?"

"Well, no, Rob. Sharon doesn't live here."

"Oh." His voice fell. "I don't suppose you have her number."

"Rob, I'm sure you are a nice man so please don't take offense, but, Sharon is a lovely girl and I really think it is up to her whether she gives out her phone number. You understand."

"You are so absolutely right," said Rob. "Why didn't I ask her for her number on Sunday?"

She laughed, "Maybe you need lessons, young man."

"Yeah, you're right. Well, I guess I'll just have to wait until next Sunday. Thanks, anyway. I've taken too much of your time."

"You're welcome."

"Just one more thing … if you happen to see Sharon, would you please tell her I called. Oh, and would you like to write down my phone number, just in case?"

"Good idea. Go ahead."

Rob gave her his number and thanked her profusely. "I'll see you on Sunday."

~~~~~

Sharon Calls Him

Rob had a few more things to do today. One was to check in with the insurance company about the rotten egg damage. He needed to submit the two bills. Also, he had to deal with Totten's lawyer. His car would be ready this afternoon, as well. He would have to ask Mom to drive him over to pick up his car. For now, he could step outside and check-out the brick cleaning job.

But first, he walked into the kitchen to refill his coffee that had gone cold. In the kitchen, he wrote a note on the slate, "Mom, can you give me a ride this afternoon, about 4PM?" With luck, Nan would be home from work by then, or maybe not. Rob wasn't sure of her hours. Boy, he was out of touch with his family. And so, he reached onto the slate and rubbed out the word Mom, replacing it with "Joy or Mom." Joy was still in bed, lucky girl.

The bricks were looking almost like new. The only problem was that the front of the house looked cleaner than the sides and back. The insurance company would not pay to have the whole house cleaned, only the front. Well, Rob would take that up with old man Totten's lawyer. Clearly Totten was more than anxious to keep this incident quiet, Rob thought, ruefully. He planned to wring Totten for as much money as possible.

Rob's phone vibrated in his pocket. He pulled it out and looked at the display which read "unknown caller." *Darn it, everybody in the world has my number, now. More idiot robo-calls!* He watched while it automatically went to voice mail. His thumb pushed the speaker button. "Hello Rob," said a female voice. "This is Sharon. I understand you tried to call me. Here's my number ..."

"Thank you God!" Rob shouted, with a fist pump and air jump. "Wah-Hoo!"

~~~~~

Tip Line-Slows

The Des Plaines police department had hundreds of calls on their tip line. Sarl's message was merely added to the list to turn over to the Chicago police department, which had been following up any tips that were clearly in their area. However, they had plenty of murder and assault cases of their own to investigate. Lending a hand for the Des Plaines police was something they tried to do, when they had time. They would not process this list until tomorrow.

~~~~~

The Crooked Judge

Meanwhile a well-dressed attorney was applying for special access with the executive assistant to Judge Malik Faakhir. The judge's office suite was in a towering downtown skyscraper. The elevator opened to a plush outer office on the 65th floor.

"Good afternoon, Fadl," said the attorney by way of greeting. "Is the judge available?"

Fadl glanced meaningfully at the clock on the wall. "It's Ase, right now. He will probably be at prayer. Is it something I can handle for you?"

"Oh, of course, I'm sorry. Please don't bother the judge. Uhm, I think you can probably get his signature on this later."

"All right let me see what you have."

"I've already prepared the document. It is a writ for the release of one J. M. Muhammad Mutawassit, who is being held without charges in the federal jail. We need to get this innocent man released immediately."

"Of course," said Fadl. "Just leave it on the corner of my desk. I will take care of it in just a few minutes."

The well-dressed attorney placed a legal sized envelope on the desk, as directed. Inside the sealed envelope a large treasury note was paper-clipped to the document.

Outside on the steps, the attorney spoke a quick message into his smart phone. "It's done as requested. Your package will be delivered within the hour."

~~~~~

Disguise

The receiving phone beeped, indicating an incoming message. Kabandha pressed a button and read the message. She nodded with satisfaction. "It's time," she said. "You know what to do."

Mohammad had prepared carefully. This time he would not fail. He armed himself with several choices of weapon. He would only use the gun as a last resort. This must be done quickly and quietly, before George had a chance to slip away. "I'll call a taxi," he said.

"No! You fool!" said Kabandha. "Cabs keep records. Records can be traced."

"Well, then, how?"

"We've gone over this before. Can't you remember anything I teach you?"

Muhammad hung his head.

"All right, then, listen to me. You must stay out of sight. Take the elevated, and then the bus, and subway downtown, then walk to the jail. Have you got that?"

"Yes, Kabandha, I think so."

"Let me see what you have on."

Mohammad walked into the room to show her.

"Oh, hell, look at you. You can't go out like that. Your description is all over the airways."

"What can I do? I can't help how I look," he whined.

"Of course you can. Have you no imagination? Come here, you stupid oaf."

Mohammad walked closer. Kabandha reached into a drawer and pulled out a kit. Opening the kit she selected a jar of stage makeup. "Hold out your hands," she ordered. She smeared the very dark brown makeup on his hands and face. Pawing through a collection of fake hair pieces she selected a wig made of long black dreadlocks. "Put this on."

Mohammad meekly obeyed.

"Now wear this." She held out a dark gray hooded sweatshirt.

"But it's in the middle of the summer, Kabandha," Mohammad protested.

She paused thinking. "You're right. We don't want you to stand out." She rose and walked over to a small wardrobe and looked through his available garments. "Here, put this on." It was a long-sleeved ratty-looking t-shirt with a sagging neckline. "I'll have to cover up your neck." She grabbed the makeup again. "Hold up your chin." She smeared some more on the exposed skin. "All right, turn around and let me see you."

Mohammad turned once around.

"That will do," she nodded in satisfaction. "Do you have all your weapons?"

Mohammad patted here and there on his person. "Yeah," he said.

"Money? Change?"

Mohammad reached into his pocket and pulled out his cash.

"Those bills are too big. You need something smaller, and plenty of coins for the machines." She reached into a drawer and thrust some bills and change into his hands.

Mohammad put it into his pocket and stood there waiting.

"Go do your thing. Get out of here," she waved him off. "And when you're home, I'll have your favorite supper ready."

Thinking about the meal to come, Mohammad said, "I'll be back for that." He walked out and closed the door.

"Not very likely," she thought.

~~~~~

Writ

Cliff Side picked up his desk phone. "Yeah."

"Get over to the jail right away."

"What's up?"

"Some judge has issued a writ to spring our boy."

"Oh shit!"

"Yup."

"On my way," said Cliff. He strapped on his firearm, and grabbed his jacket.

~~~~~

Sprung & Shot

At the jail, George looked up when he heard the key turning in the lock. A guard opened his cell door, "You," he pointed. "Come with me."

They walked down the row of cells and into the outer offices. "Wait right there." The man retrieved a large envelope containing George's possessions and handed it to him. "Here's your stuff. You're free to go."

George was dumbfounded, but wasn't about to ask questions.

"Out that door." The guard pointed and turned back to his work.

George opened the door and walked out into the sunshine on the front steps of the jail. He stood there blinking for a moment wondering what to do next. He opened his wallet to see if he had any money. Son-of-a-gun, his money was still there. Okay, well then, he might as well start walking. Maybe he could get something to eat and then call someone to come pick him up. No, that wasn't a good idea. It would be better to hide for a while until he figured out his next move. He had enough cash for a hotel room.

George started walking briskly down the steps, turning right on the sidewalk. Everything about the city looked normal, sounded normal. Traffic hummed by as usual. Nothing seemed out of order. Whistling a little tune, George walked along the shops and offices, looking for a place to eat, unaware of the muffled steps closing in behind him.

He turned down a side street that seemed promising. Ah, here was a good-looking place to eat. "Ugh," suddenly he bent over grabbing his side. His breath escaped in a rush. His brain barely had time to register alarm. It happened so fast he did not feel the dagger enter between his ribs, turn and rip his lungs before it sliced his aorta. George's heart took one last beat and stopped. He slumped to his knees and sprawled on the sidewalk. Eyes rolled up in their sockets, red blood slowly seeping into his t-shirt.

Mohammad sank into the shadows and watched to be certain the knife did its job. Satisfied he turned to scurry away. "Hold it right there," yelled Cliff. "Don't move!"

Mohammad's head jerked toward the voice as his hand went for his gun. Shots rang out.

~~~~~

Mail Call

Back in Arlington, Sally Millecan, nee Miller, carefully filed her two birth certificates away in the lockbox, pulled a chair over to her closet, climbed up and stored the lockbox away on a high shelf. Stepping down, she stood back and looked at it for a second. As she closed the closet door she vowed to close her mind on the issue, as well. She had learned all she could and probably would never know anything about her father. Her mother was still suffering too much from the memories. Sally doubted they could ever discuss it again.

Of course, Sally regretted having pushed her mother into having one of her terror attacks. It was awful—so sad. However, because of her questions, Sally learned that Miller was her real name, and how it been changed to Millecan. Now she knew that her mother had changed it herself by altering the birth certificate. Some time afterward, Ferrell must have begun using the new name of Millecan for both of them.

Sally had no idea how Ferrell Millecan legally entered Canada. The incorrect spelling of her mother's name on the altered certificate must have just been a mistake. Ferrell must have somehow changed her own name from Miller to Millecan in order to get the proper ID to cross the border. Of course, in those days, a mere driver's license was accepted as sufficient ID at the border. *Well, there I go again,* Sally berated herself. Her brain would not let go. The thoughts replayed over and over in her mind—those facts she knew, along with the remaining unanswered questions. She could drive herself crazy.

This was the first chance she had to think through what to do about her name. Should she change it back to Miller? She considered all the entities that would be affected, from utility bills to credit cards and online names. What a mess!

For now, Sally decided to continue being Sally Millecan. The possibility of losing her job over a name mixup was enough to frighten her. So long as Sally Millecan continued to have the proper security clearance, she had better not rock the boat.

Sally had tomorrow off. It would be good to catch up on her laundry and housework, and do banking and shopping. Tonight she planned to turn in early and read in bed for a while until she got sleepy. She looked forward to reading that Western romance novel she picked up at the airport store in Victoria. It was just the sort of escape reading she needed right now.

One last time, she checked her email messages, scrolling down through the junk mail finding nothing of importance. Her paper mail was still on the desk. She strolled over, stood at her desk, picked up the mail and casually sorted it out, using the four-pile system: Pile one—open now, pile two—bills, three—magazines and four—open later. The rest went into the waste basket. She hated this job.

Although she loved her Arlington apartment where she could relax and be herself, the one thing she hated was coming home to a stack of mail, even though most of it was junk, advertisements and appeals for charity.

Once a month she got a paycheck from her lobbyist employer. It should have been in this pile of mail. It always came right on time. Sally went through the piles again, looking for the familiar envelope. *It should be here. Did I throw it away?* Sally started digging through the wastebasket. *Oh here it is. How did I miss that?*

Kicking herself, Sally pulled out the desk chair and sat down to open the envelope and prepare the check for deposit. She read the little sticky note attached to the check. "We need 2 meet. Starbucks' at 10? Email me when ur in town, EJM." *Shucks there goes half my morning.* She had to meet Edward tomorrow morning. Sally sighed. *Oh well, stuff happens.* She dashed off a quick note to Edward, grabbed her novel and headed toward the bedroom, telling herself to take no thought for the morrow as today's concerns were sufficient for the day.

~~~~~

Starbucks Edward

Edward was waiting for her. He stood when Sally entered. Such a gentleman, she thought. Handsome, too. *I wish he would ask me out on a date, sometime.*

"Good morning," said Edward.

"Good morning," she smiled.

Edward pulled out her chair and helped her into her seat.

"Thank you," said Sally. "How are you today?"

"Doing well, thank you," Edward replied, "And you?"

Their personal conversation never went beyond polite greetings. Sally wondered about the slight accent Edward had. She could usually place voices, as she heard people from all over the world, in her day job. Edward's voice had her stumped. She would like to ask him about his family, job, background etc. but she knew that was verboten.

Edward had chosen a table that was set off from the others. He lowered his voice and got right down to business. "We need to go over your work for the next few days," he began.

"Is everything all right? I hope there is no problem," she said. Truthfully, she thought that her reports were a waste of time, for which she was being overpaid. She braced herself for the news, whether good or bad.

"No problem whatsoever," Edward assured her. "We are happy that you have gotten acquainted with the right people. You have done well."

"Well, okay, if you are happy, that's all that matters. I admit I don't understand any of it."

"No need to understand. We just follow orders. Who cares, so long as the client pays the big bucks?" He laughed. "I'm told that we are to proceed with the next phase of the operation."

"Oh?"

"They have selected the most likely target and want you to pinpoint the targeted person and hire him to work for us."

"What? Are you kidding?"

"Not at all, and there is good news."

"Good news?"

"Good news for you, that is."

"Okay, I can use some good news."

"This will be a step-up for you in terms of your salary."

"That is really good news!" she was excited.

Motioning with one hand, Edward reminded her to keep her voice down. "From now on you will be on my level, salary-wise."

Sally knew that more money meant more responsibility. "And so, what do I have to do to qualify for this new level?"

"You will be a contact person, just like me."

"I don't understand."

"Well, I am your contact, right?"

"One of them," Sally answered, thinking about the young girl.

Edward raised an eyebrow. This was new information to him. Disregarding that for the moment, he continued, "You will be the contact person for the new employee. You will meet him on the DC to Dallas flight occasionally."

"I see," said Sally, although she really did not see at all.

"At those times, you will merely pass on the message."

"That's all?"

"Yup, easy."

"I don't have to take pictures and send reports on the various people, anymore?"

"No, I think they have selected one. You have done a good job. And so now, all you have to do is pass on messages to that particular person."

"Who is it?"

"I don't even know that, myself."

Sally was feeling uncomfortable about this new arrangement. It sounded like it was right out of one of those spy novels she loved to read. This was no longer a game. But, how could she get out of it? She needed the money for a few more months. As soon as possible she would resign, that's for sure.

"Okay," said Sally, "I'll do it for a while at least, but I'm not committing to forever."

"Excellent, I hoped you would say that. We don't need forever."

"I suppose that someone else will tell me how to identify this person."

"Actually, I don't think so. He has been told to look for you."

"Oh."

"You will receive a password which he will know as well. That is how you will find each other."

Yikes, thought Sally. *This is getting weirder and weirder.*

"And then, you will receive his answer."

"His answer ... right. Do I know the question?"

"No need to know the question. He will give you his answer and you will report it back to us in the usual way.

"I've taken care of the check," said Edward as he abruptly stood. "It's been pleasant. I'll bid you good-day."

Sally stared after him as he left. Who was this guy? Sometimes his wording was peculiar. Could English be his second language? *Oh wait, he never gave me the password.* Sally sighed. Her nature was to be curious. It was so hard to be patient when you did not understand.

Chapter 12 Zip-a-dee-do-da

n his way over to the McGillicuddy residence for dinner, Rob had the top down on his freshly cleaned convertible. A tune kept going through his mind.

"Zip-ah-dee-do-da, zip-ah-dee-a,

My oh my what a beautiful day.

Plenty of sunshine, comin' my way

Dah-da-da, dah-da ... "

What were the rest of the words? Rob couldn't think where this was coming from. Sounded like an old Walt Disney movie.

He was invited to Sharon's aunt and uncle's house for dinner. Golly, he hardly knew her and already he was meeting her folks. Or, maybe the idea was for them to look him over. He wasn't even sure that Sharon would be there, but who was he to complain? If their approval was a requirement, no biggie. He could handle that.

Rob was dressed in a suit, shirt and tie. He even got a haircut and shoeshine. It had been a long time since he had dressed up for a girl, much less for her aunt and uncle.

Parking at the curb, he used a little squirt of mouth freshener, checked his teeth and necktie in the mirror, picked up the bouquet of flowers laying on the seat, and opened the car door. Walking up the sidewalk toward the front of the house, he felt butterflies. *Come on, Rob, get a grip. It's only a girl you just met.*

He rang the doorbell and waited, nervously tapping his toe and whistling the rest of the tune. A jovial middle-aged gentleman answered the door, "Good evening."

"Good evening, I'm Rob Goodrich. Uh ..."

"Rob! Hello. Please come in. I'm Sharon's Uncle Terry." He held the door open. "Call me Terry," he said. "Welcome to our home." He ushered Rob through a slate-tiled hall, decorated with a gilded mirror, a small half table on one wall and framed art across from it. An open staircase went off to one side. A long crystal chandelier hung down from the second floor shining through tall windows to the outside.

"Come along with me," said Terry. "Let me make you comfortable in the living room." He led Rob through an archway into a well-appointed room. "May I take care of those flowers for you, Rob?"

"Oh yes, thank you," said Rob, handing him the bouquet.

"I assume these are for the lady of the house," Terry smiled.

Rob nodded. "Uh, yeah."

"I'll see that Rose gets these, right away. Why don't you make yourself comfortable anywhere you like, and I'll let Sharon know you're here. All right?"

"Thank you, Terry," said Rob, unable to think of anything brilliant to say. *Wasn't it better to allow Terry to wonder if I might be stupid than to open my mouth and prove him right?* Instead Rob displayed his brilliant smile, prepared to select a chair and sit down to wait.

"Excuse me, then," said Terry. "Hopefully Sharon will be here any minute."

Rob knew her phone number now, but he had no idea where she lived. He had heard of girls meeting men at a neutral restaurant for a first date, but this was novel. He would have to teach his sister about this trick. If Joy had used it on her first date with that Totten s.o.b, he would never have passed the test.

Just then Rob heard the doorbell again followed by feminine footsteps going down the hall. Soon he heard two women talking and laughing in the foyer. Were they laughing about him? Rob stood in place when Sharon and her aunt entered the room. "Hi Rob," said Sharon. "Sorry I'm late. Have you waited long?"

"Not long at all. I only just arrived myself."

"That's good. Aunt Rose, I'd like you to meet my friend from church, Rob Goodrich. Rob, this is my Aunt Rose."

"How do you do, Rob? I believe we have talked on the phone," said Rose, extending her right hand.

Rob took her hand. "Delighted to meet you, ma'am," said Rob. "Yes, I did call here trying to track down your lovely niece."

"Well, it seems you were successful," said Rose.

"Indeed, I was very lucky to find her," said Rob, "and happy to be invited to your beautiful home."

"You are more than welcome, Rob, and thank you for the flowers. Very nice, indeed. I've arranged them for the table."

"You are welcome."

"Now, if you'll excuse me, I have a few things to attend to. I'll leave you two to enjoy yourselves. Dinner will be in about half an hour."

Rob nodded.

Sharon asked, "Is there anything I can do to help, Aunt Rose?"

"Yes, dear, you can entertain our guest."

Sharon turned to Rob. "Shall we sit over here?" She indicated a love seat, across the room.

"Okay."

Sharon took his hand and led him to the seat. She sat first. Rob followed, as close as he dared, still holding her hand. They grinned at each other. "Well, what do you think of my parents?"

"I'm sure they are lovely people," said Rob, "but never having met them, I can only judge from having met their wonderful daughter."

Sharon's laugh tinkled like a bell. "You just met them, silly."

"Oh?"

"Yes, my aunt and uncle raised me from the age of six."

"Ah, I see. And so this is your home, where you were raised."

"Partly. We moved once, but I lived here from about the age of twelve on, until I grew up and left for school."

"So, do you remember your parents?"

"Yes, I remember some things. I was six when they died, but Aunt Rose made every effort to help me remember, with pictures and stories. And so, I'm not always sure if it is my own memory or something I was told. It sort-of all runs together."

"Not sure if I should say 'I'm sorry'," Rob commented.

Sharon laughed a little and then sighed. "I know. That's okay. Aunt Rose and Uncle Terry still insist I call them aunt and uncle, but to me they are my parents. That's what I remember the most."

"Uhm."

"Was that your car I saw in the drive?" she asked, changing the subject.

"Yes, I just got it out of the shop this afternoon."

"My, what a change since the last time I saw it!"

"Yeah, Scott's Body Shop did a good job. It's never been this clean since it was new." Rob laughed.

"You were happy with the settlement?"

"Uh, you mean the insurance company?"

"No, I mean Judge Totten's."

"Not sure about that."

"What did he tell you?"

"I haven't talked with Judge Totten."

"He told me he would pay you double."

"Told you?" Rob wondered what on earth he had missed. "How did that happen? Did you talk to Totten?"

"Why, of course. Don't you know we officers always get our man?"

"You did that?"

"Didn't you read the report?"

"I didn't even see any report. All I could get out of the police was a big fat yawn."

"Really?"

"Honey, they won't tell me anything."

"Aw, geez, I'm sorry."

"Me too."

"Well, how about taking me out after dinner for a buggy ride in that nice clean car of yours?"

"I'd love to, but there is only one problem, there isn't room for four people."

Sharon laughed, "That's the idea."

Rob thought, *I guess I passed the test.*

~~~~~

Kabandha Waits.

Glued to the television set, Kabandha waited impatiently for the late evening news. She knew something had happened. Otherwise Mohammad would have been back by now. The special dinner was dried and ruined, long since gone cold, sitting in the oven. Kabandha pushed aside any feelings of regret, assuring herself that Mohammad and George would both give freely of themselves—heroes for the cause. Allah would richly reward them in heaven.

At ten o'clock the Chicago news coverage droned on covering the latest political scandal, citing quotes and short clips of various opinionated pompous asses. Then it tilted to weather and sports, with long interruptions for commercials selling all manner of devices and drugs to the decadent morons of society watching this drivel. Wouldn't they ever get to the important information?

Finally, at the end a brief announcement: "Chicago area citizens can relax and go about their normal lives. The Holiday Inn killer has been shot in a confrontation with authorities. Chief Adkins of the Des Plaines police hailed the officer who made the shot as a hero."

Kabandha spat. "Hero! Pah! My Mohammad is the one deserving of praise. He is the hero—shot in cold blood while carrying out his duty to Allah."

Kabandha booted up her laptop and went to the special web site. Reading through the twitter site, she checked to see if there any news from her group. She checked out the obituaries list lauding the heroes who have sacrificed themselves for the cause. It was amazing to see how widespread the work had become. People from all corners of the world were joining the ji-had.

It would be up to her, now, to make sure that their sacrifices had counted for something. She would carry on their mission. Kabandha had a plan.

Chapter 13 Next Day

Nate and Cliff Wrap. Mohammad Under Arrest

liff looked up from his desk as Nate walked in and tossed his hat onto a peg. "What are you doing here?" he grumped.

"Good morning, friend," said Nate. "Aren't you happy to see me?"

Cliff picked up his coffee cup and leaned back in his desk chair, narrowing his eyes at Nate. "Seems to me you've caused me enough trouble."

"Who me?" Nate held up his hands, palms forward. He pulled up a side chair and sat next to Cliff's desk.

"Look at this pile," said Cliff pointing at a tall stack of papers and reports. "You have no idea what it's like, do you?"

"Umm, I guess not."

"Haven't you ever shot somebody?"

"That's classified information," laughed Nate.

"Reports, bah-humbug. I have to account for every last bullet fired from my gun... in triplicate."

"And here I thought the media was playing you up as a hero."

"Yeah, right. No hero. I just shot a private citizen."

"Who happens to be a terrorist, who is wanted for double murder," Nate reminded him.

"Who is innocent until proven guilty," grumbled Cliff.

"According to his lawyer representative who was only too eager to go before the cameras and claim that the evil Chicago cops are profiling and targeting minorities, again. This time it's innocent, law-abiding Muslims."

"Never mind it was a Federal Agent who shot the guy, and not a Chicago cop," Cliff moaned.

"Details," said Nate with a chuckle. "I don't suppose you've got anything out of the victim of your 'irresponsible' shooting?"

"Naw, we can't even get near him. Chicago cops got him under wraps."

"How bad is he?"

"I guess they don't expect him to make it," Cliff sighed.

"In which case, you may get a paid holiday while justice slowly grinds."

Cliff shrugged. "I'm already assigned to this desk, writing up my report. Make that plural."

"We also serve who sit and write." Nate laughed.

"Come on, give me a break."

"Speaking of breaks, how about breakfast? I'm buying."

Cliff gave him a meaningful look and stood up. "You're on."

~~~~~

Nate Studies New Pics

Flying home, Nate watched the suburbs of Chicago fade into the distance as the plane approached the wide-open spaces of the prairie and beyond to the mountains. He closed his eyes, relaxed and snoozed.

Opening his eyes he glanced at his watch. An hour had passed. *Damn it would feel good to get home and put all this Chicago trip behind him.*

Nate reached for the purple briefcase he carried with him this time. Although he was off-duty, he was still a Federal Air Marshal. Being off-duty made it okay to nap. But inside the briefcase were three days of directives that he needed to study. It was time to catch up.

Reflecting back on his time with Cliff, he appreciated the time spent with an old friend. No doubt the Chicago branch of the Air Marshal service could finish up the case. Nate had left it in good hands. Hopefully they would round up the entire terrorist cell—one less terrorist for Nate to worry about.

~~~~~

Rob Gets a Call

"Morning Miss Sharon," greeted the jolly man assigned to the desk this day.

"Hey, Papa Buck, how ya' doin'?" Buck Boyles was a favorite of all the young cops at the precinct. He was nearing retirement, and so he only worked part-time. But, when he was on duty, he never failed to remember their names and birthdays.

"I'm just peachy-dandy," said Buck, his wide grin displaying a few missing teeth, testimony to his hard years as a beat cop. "And how are you doing, Miss Sharon? Found yourself a handsome boyfriend yet?"

"Aw, come on, Papa, I don't need a man."

Buck chuckled, "Sure you do. I keep telling ya' the right man can solve all your problems."

"More like cause me more problems, Papa."

"Now, you listen to me, young lady, I can fix you right up."

"Well, Papa, actually there is something you can do for me."

"A favor?"

"Yes."

"Great! I'm into favors. Just the thing I need." He slapped his hand on his leg and grinned at her.

"It's just a little thing, but would you mind making a phone call for me?"

"Sure, baby. Lay it on me."

"Well, it's a case I worked on, a misdemeanor. It was just vandalism to his house and car. But, the victim needs to hear that the case is resolved. That's all."

"Um, I see," said Buck with a twinkle in his eye. "And this victim... could he possibly be a handsome young man?"

Sharon blushed. "Of course not. Whatever made you think that?"

Buck chuckled, knowingly.

"He is just a private citizen who deserves better treatment from our department. Just a phone call, that's all, I swear," Sharon insisted.

Buck sighed. "Give me his name and number."

"Thank's Papa, I owe you."

"Make those donuts chocolate with sprinkles, please."

~~~~~

Rob Deals with Lawyer

Beetle and Bailey, LLC, proclaimed the gilt letters on the office door. When Rob opened the door, a soft tone announced his arrival. He walked across thick carpet to a solid cherry reception desk. The beautiful young women at the desk was dressed in expensive professional attire, a black tailored suit and white silk blouse. Her hair was coifed in a chignon. Her nails were groomed and painted a discrete rose tone that matched her lips. If Rob had been closer he would have gotten a whiff of Chanel Number 5. "Good afternoon, sir, may I help you?"

"Good afternoon. My name is Robert Goodrich. I'm here about the Totten offer."

"Oh yes, Mr. Goodrich, I have the papers right here for you to sign. But, Mr. Lawrence would like to speak with you first. Can you wait just a moment while I let him know you are here?"

"Yes, of course."

She lifted a slim phone and pressed a button. "Mr. Goodrich is here to see you, sir." She paused, clicked off and informed Rob. "He'll be right out. Would you care for something? We have coffee, water or soda."

"Thank you, no. I'm good," said Rob.

"Then if you'll just have a seat, it may be a moment."

"Thanks, I'll stand." Rob joined his hands behind his back and began a tour of the expensive art on the walls.

Soon a thirty-something man approached wearing a dark suit with a tiny pinstripe, polished shoes and a designer tie. "Mr. Goodrich, I presume?"

"Yes."

"Hello, I'm Justin Lawrence." He extended a hand. "Nice to meet you."

"Thank you," said Rob. "I'm here about the Totten offer."

"Yes, I can help you with that." He picked up the contract papers from the front desk. "Shall we step into this office?" He held a door open for Rob and gestured him inside.

The office was bare except for a beautiful polished wood conference table, eight plush chairs and original art on every wall. "Just sit anywhere," said Lawrence. Rob selected a chair at the end and Lawrence chose one on the corner. "Now, I presume you have had a chance to look-over this offer, right?"

"No, as a matter of fact, we have not heard anything since we sent you the copies of our bills," Rob answered.

"Well, in that case let me give you a brief run-down of the terms, and then you can look it over yourself. Judge Totten has made what we think is a very generous offer. He has agreed to pay you double your damages. In return you need to accept that as suitable and agree to a non-disclosure agreement and to drop any charges, either criminal or civil."

"I see," said Rob.

"And so, assuming that is acceptable to you, would you like to read the agreement? If you sign It today, we are authorized to issue your check immediately and you can be on your way."

"Not just yet."

"Is there some problem?" His voice was incredulous. "As I said, we believe this is a more than generous offer and the terms are quite standard, I assure you."

"Yes, it would be generous, except that more damage has come to light."

Mr. Lawrence's face fell. "How can there be more damage?"

"Well, my car is fine. No problem there. It was cleaned and repainted. It's the house. After the front had a chance to dry completely from the cleaning operation, we saw that the color of the bricks had changed. As a result they no longer match the rest of the house. Our cleaning and restoration company is considered the best in the city. They assured us that this result was typical, because of the chemical reaction of the cleaning fluid. There is a special fluid that is required to remove eggs."

"Did they say what could be done to make it all match?"

"Well, the new color is good enough. The only problem is that it is different, now, from the rest of the house. The restoration company said the only solution was to treat the entire house with the same chemical."

"And can they guarantee it will match?"

"No, but they have had success in other cases."

"And the cost?"

"The area to be treated is approximately five times the size of the front."

"I see."

Rob waited.

"And the rest of the terms? Are they agreeable?"

"Yes, assuming they are as you say, we have no reason to ruin the Totten boy's reputation. That is, assuming, of course, that he has remorse and will not bother us any further, nor will he make any new remarks or write any derogatory statements about anyone in my family, including and especially my sister."

"Um, we may need to add those conditions to the contract."

Rob waited.

"Well, what do you anticipate will be the cost of these further repairs?"

Rob mentioned a figure.

"Ah, well, that is a little more than we are authorized to go, at this point. However, what you present seems reasonable. I will get back to my client with this new amount and new conditions, and phone you. Will tomorrow be soon enough?"

"Yes, and please send me the new contract by email or fax as soon as it is ready. I will need to have our lawyer look at it."

"Very well," said Mr. Lawrence. "Thank you for coming in."

Rob stood and offered his hand. "Good day, Mr. Lawrence."

~~~~~

Sally Gets the Password.

Now that she had this promotion, Sally knew she would have to be on the DC-Dallas-Seattle flight more often. Like the rest of the flight attendants, Sally preferred the direct flights and so she probably would have no trouble getting the Virgin American assignment. Even though adding the Dallas stop made for a much longer day, it had the advantage of paying more. There were pros and cons to everything.

Sally wondered how this new assignment would work out.

Edward made it sound simple enough, but Sally had her doubts. Well, there was only one way to find out and that was to just do it. Sally picked up her flight bag, grabbed the handle of her roll-aboard and headed out the door.

Sitting at her regular table, Sally dug into a hearty late breakfast. She wouldn't have much time to eat once she got busy on the plane. No need to watch for her contact, the young girl knew where to find her. Instead, Sally was surprised when Edward pulled out a chair and sat opposite her. Sally gasped, "Oh," and then quickly composed her features. "Hi," she said.

Edward had one thing to say, "The words to watch for are 'bacon and eggs'."

"Like this," Sally gestured at her plate of bacon and eggs.

Edward nodded.

"Bacon and eggs," Sally repeated the words silently.

Edward nodded, stood up, pushed in his chair, turned and disappeared into the crowd.

~~~~~

The Flight

Virgin American Airlines flight #1715 departed Reagan International, right on time. The flight attendants remained buckled in until the plane was airborne. Sally had greeted each and every first-class passenger by name, with no idea which one would be her target. Maybe he wasn't even on the plane today.

She smiled and made idle chit-chat with her companion flight attendants, as they worked in the galley, preparing the meals. Once the flight leveled out at altitude, Sally began taking orders from her passengers. She greeted each one, in turn. "Hello, Mr. or hello, Ms. We have several choices for lunch today," and then she would go through the menu choices: beef, chicken or vegetarian. After years of practice, Sally was able to remember each passenger's choice, with rare exceptions. She had a way of matching the seat numbers with the letters, B, C, or V.

All was going well until she approached seat #6A.

"I would like bacon and eggs," said a quite normal looking man, average actually. Pale brown eyes looked directly at her. The only thing that gave him away was the nervous drumming of his fingers on his seat tray.

Sally stopped short, glancing at his hands.

The man quickly clasped them in his lap.

"I wish we had some bacon and eggs for you," said Sally, quietly. "That sounds good right now, doesn't it?"

"Well, in that case, the chicken will do," he said.

"Certainly, sir," said Sally and calmly looked over at the party in the window seat. "And what will you have, ma'am?"

Out over Texas, Sally had a chance to visit with a few of the passengers. Her target man was somewhat of a surprise to her, as she had met him before and gotten to know him as some kind of computer software engineer working at a small tech firm supplying the airplane industry. She tried to remember the name of the firm and what they did. The details escaped her. Why do you suppose this man was a target, and for what purpose? Sally paused at his seat and smiled. "I hope you are enjoying your flight, Mr. Brown," she offered.

"Indeed I am," he responded. "Ah … I don't suppose you would have time-off between flights?"

So there it was—the contact offer.

She laughed, trying to cover her dismay while she thought of what to say. "Um, well, as you know this flight continues on to Seattle."

"Oh, yes, I know, but there is a change of planes. Right?"

"Yes, it continues on Alaska Airlines. I don't always work that flight."

"Today?"

"Um…" she stalled. "I'll have to check." Sally moved on down the aisle.

After all the passengers deplaned, Sally followed the rest of the crew up the ramp. They would soon scatter to their respective lives. Sally paused at the gate, looking around. Sure enough, someone sat in a darkened corner of the lounge. It was him. Sally nodded slightly, in acknowledgment, turned and moved off toward the terminal. She needed to make this look like a casual, happenstance meeting.

Unsure how to arrange this she continued walking, searching for a quiet secluded restaurant, of which none existed. Bright lights were everywhere. And then she remembered there was a certain bar-type lounge in the main terminal. Perhaps that would work. How could she do this? *Think, Sally.*

Just then, she felt a tap on her shoulder. Startled, she reflexed, turned and quickly inhaled.

"Excuse me," said Mr. Brown. "I seem to be lost."

143

Recovering quickly Sally asked, "Where are you trying to go?"

"I need to pick up my luggage and get a taxicab to my hotel," he laughed. "I must have made a wrong turn."

"I don't think I can help you, sir," said Sally.

"You must know the way to the baggage claim," he remarked.

"Well, to tell you the truth, I've never needed that particular place," she laughed, "but surely the overhead signs will point the way. Don't you think?"

"The answer is 'yes' and you can report that," he said.

"Got it," she nodded.

"Good," he said and left her standing there.

Chapter 14 Kabandha

Kabandha Decides to Sabotage

*O*nly a few of her co-conspirators knew Kabandha's true identity and training. She had a graduate degree in computer science with an emphasis in cyber security and software engineering. Only a few women were on this career path and even fewer of them were minorities. Kabandha had worked extremely hard for many years to achieve this status. Moreover she had carefully avoided any marks on her record and thus was able to qualify for top secret clearance to work herself up to some of the most sensitive projects for the government.

Her recent enviable assignment was in research and development for the FAA (Federal Aviation Administration). One of their projects had been in the works for years. They were attempting to develop a system that would enhance and eventually replace the current air traffic control system which identifies the positions of aircraft with radar and transponders. Those positions are shown on complex display screens which air traffic controllers watch and use to direct traffic coast to coast and around the world as well.

This new system, known as the ACAS X (pronounced A-Kass-Ex) would also replace the TCAS system which was currently in place on commercial airliners all over the world. TCAS (pronounced T'-kass) requires all planes over a certain size to continuously and automatically broadcast their GPS position. All newly manufactured airplanes and any older airplanes which were retrofitted with input receivers could identify all the aircraft in their vicinity and display them on a screen in the cockpit.

Interestingly, anyone within range on the ground with such a receiver could display the signals as easily as could an aircraft. Kabandha was one of the few who knew about this 'Achilles heel' in the system. She had apps on her smart phone and all her computer devices that could display all the airplanes overhead within a certain radius. She enjoyed sitting in her room and watching what was going on overhead.

Eventually, the FAA's goal was to develop software which would be able to essentially take-over control of the plane in case of emergency such as an impending collision whether that be a mountain, plane, land or sea. This would replace the pilot's slower human response to impending collisions, thus allowing far less spacing between planes approaching busy air space. With the limited number of airports and the steadily increasing number of airplanes in the sky, it was important to be able to crowd them closer together.

It would be years before such a system was completely in place, but Kabandha knew that her company was working on a prototype which was undergoing tests, ready for a third test out of Chicago in two or three days' time.

Kabandha intended to be there. She had another idea of a secret test that she wanted to make.

~~~~~

Cops Raid Her Apt. Too Late.

But, first, she knew she could be in danger, so long as she stayed in this apartment. Both of those worthless men had gotten themselves in trouble with the authorities. They knew nothing of importance, except of course her location and name. They did not know about her day job and education. For all they knew she was just an overgrown bossy female who didn't know her place.

Kabandha snorted. Ha! George and Mohammad were useless to her now. But, she was worried about what the police may have squeezed out of these weaklings before they were wasted. Kabandha needed to leave. She began packing her things and erasing all traces of her presence from the apartment. No clue to her identity could be left behind.

Carrying an oversized tote bag, and pulling two heavy pullman-sized suitcases, she was ready to leave by early morning. It was a struggle without her men to help, but Kabandha was a much stronger woman than most people would think. She had to destroy any trail, and so she walked for several minutes before she got on a city bus. She rode for many blocks toward the center of the city, before disembarking from this bus and catching another cross town. Eventually she would find a room to rent somewhere closer to her place of business.

~~~~~

Tip Line Follow-Up

Too late, the Chicago police sent an ordinary beat cop to check out the nosy neighbor's tip. He parked a marked cruiser out front and walked up one flight to apartment 2B. He rang the bell first and then banged on the door loudly. Across the hall, Sari listened. Scurrying to the window she saw the cruiser parked out front. Back to her door, she eased it open a notch so she could watch. When the uniformed cop turned to leave, she quickly closed it, hoping to remain unseen. Clearly no one was answering the door.

After a few minutes the cop turned away, went back to his cruiser, reported in and drove off.

~~~~~

Home Never Felt Better

"Honey, I'm home," Nate called as he set his bag down in the foyer. No one answered. Nate glanced at his watch, only 1:30 PM. Of course, Nan was still at work. He had gained a couple of hours flying West. But, where were the kids? Well maybe the cat was home. Nate hung up his jacket, rolled up his shirt sleeves and headed for the kitchen. No doubt the cat would show herself as soon as he opened the refrigerator door.

Nate selected a tall soda for himself and a half-eaten can of cat-food for Daisy.

A three-year-old medium-haired golden tiger cat lay in her favorite spot atop the extra refrigerator in the laundry room. Hearing the kitchen fridge door open and close, she aroused from her nap and stretched.

Nate heard soft paws thump, first on the counter and then on the floor. *Here she comes*, he thought. "Hello, Daisy," he said as the warm yellow fur-ball greeted him by doing figure eights in and around his legs and crying, "Meow." As soon as Nate picked up the can of cat-food and a spoon from the drawer Daisy hot-footed over to her dish and cried up at Nate, "Meow." As Nate spooned the required ration into her dish, she could barely wait for him to finish, so anxious was she to commence eating with her usual dainty bites. "Doesn't anyone ever feed you?" he asked as she busied herself devouring her meal. "Judging by that pot-belly I see hanging down, you need to go on a diet."

Nate sat on a stool and drank his soft drink while he watched her. *God, it feels good just to be home where life is simple.* Daisy finished her repast, had a few laps of water and retired to her bed to groom her fur.

Nate took his drink into the master bedroom where he hung up his suit, put away his traveling shoes, and tossed the rest into the laundry basket.

Stepping into the shower, he turned it on hot and sharp, lathered up, stood there for a few minutes enjoying the shower massage on his tired muscles, and then rinsed with cool water. Grabbing a large soft towel he whistled as he briskly rubbed himself dry. Nate hung up the towel to dry and donned his swimming trunks and sunglasses. He grabbed another large towel and a magazine and headed out back to the pool. Looking around for a shady spot, he dragged a lounge chair over into a corner under some overhanging branches. Lowering the chair's back as far down as it would go, he spread out his towel, added a pillow, laid down and covered his eyes with the magazine. Within minutes he was asleep, at peace with the world.

~~~~~

Rob Dates Sharon

Nate was still sound asleep when Rob Goodrich and Sharon McGillicuddy entered the pool area and ran hand-in-hand toward the deep end of the pool. "Ready?" asked Rob. Sharon nodded. "Okay, on a count of three, here we go, one–two–three." They jumped in together making a huge happy splash.

Droplets fell on Nate, waking him up. At first he reached for his weapon, hitting bare skin and quickly realizing where he was. And so, the best option was to play dead and see what happened. He heard splashing coming from the water, as two heads popped up, followed by giggling and more splashing. He recognized Rob's voice and that of a girl. Was it Joy? He didn't think so, nor was it Nan.

Then there was silence. Curious, he opened one eye and turned his head so he could peek out from under the magazine. Oh, now the silence made sense. He saw his son with arms wrapped around some woman, smiling into her face. Rob kissed her and then they both sank under the water. Apparently, the two of them had no idea anyone was there. Nate quietly picked up his towel and headed into the house.

By the time the couple had finished their swim, Nate was dressed and in the kitchen preparing snacks.

"Dad! You're home!" Rob exclaimed as he stood there, his handsome body dripping water onto the kitchen floor.

"Hello, son," said Nate. "I'm fixing some snacks and two drinks for you and your date. I hope that is okay with you."

"That's wonderful, Dad, but make it three drinks. Come and join us, I want you to meet my girl." Rob wrapped a beach towel around his waist and knotted it to the side.

"Okay, I have time," said Nate.

"Just give me a minute before you come out, okay? No doubt Sharon will want to put on her coverup."

Nate chuckled, looking out the window at the pool area. A beautiful woman had just finished toweling herself off. She was dressed in a modest bikini, if there was such a thing. Nate amused himself thinking, *Isn't modest and bikini an oxymoron?* Aloud, he said, "Hmm," deciding that any comment he made at the moment would be wrong. Sometimes silence was golden.

"One minute—got it," said Nate turning to the refrigerator to add another can of soda as Rob left by the door. Nate moved back to the window staying out of sight. He could imagine what Rob was saying to the woman judging by the gestures toward the house. Rob picked up her beach coverup and offered it to her. The woman looked toward the house and quickly shimmied into it.

Nate waited a few more seconds and then he picked up the tray and headed for the sliding door into the pool area. He managed to keep his balance while he opened and closed the door without dropping anything off the tray.

Rob stood near a table and turned toward his dad with an expectant look on his face. Sharon was seated at the table, watching as Nate approached to set the tray down on the table.

"Dad, this is my girlfriend, Sharon McGillicuddy. Sharon I'd like you to meet my father, Nate Goodrich."

"Hello," said Sharon.

"Please to meet you again, Miss McGillicuddy." Nate offered his hand. "I've seen you at church many times, but have never had the pleasure of meeting you."

"Of course," said Sharon. "I've spoken with your wife, and I know your daughter well."

"Oh you know Joy?"

"Yes, we see each other at the Sunday School opening service. Sometimes she leads the singing."

"I see," said Nate, realizing that he did not know everything that went on in Joy's life.

"Here, Dad, sit down and join us," said Rob, pulling out a chair for Nate.

"Thanks, Rob. I'll enjoy that." He smiled at Sharon.

Rob sat in one of the remaining chairs and folded his hands on the table. There was a strained silence while everyone waited for someone to say something.

"Well," said Nate, filling the silence, "why don't we dig in? You choose first, Sharon. What would you like to drink?"

"This will be fine, thank you," said Sharon, choosing the water.

Rob opened a can of soda for himself. Nate took the last one. "Here, please help yourselves to some chips," Nate offered. Rob grabbed a handful and started munching. Sharon selected two chips and held them in her hand.

Nate looked at the two of them, "So, tell me, how did you two happen to meet? At church, I suppose."

"Actually, no, Dad," said Rob. "In fact, it's quite a story."

"Oh really?" asked Nate.

"How far back should I go?" Rob looked at Sharon.

"Your story, you tell it," said Sharon.

"Well, I'll start with the vandalism."

"Huh, what vandalism?" Nate said with some alarm. "I've missed something."

"It was while you were gone, Dad. No worries. It's all fixed now."

"What happened?"

"It sounds so juvenile, like a bunch of middle-schoolers, really." Rob was a bit embarrassed.

"Go on."

"Some guy came over in the middle of the night and rotten-egged my car and the house."

"Just like that? What did you do?"

"Well, maybe he thought he was getting back at me."

"How so?"

"Well, that's another story, but anyway, I thought I should call the police and report this. I mean it wasn't just a little egg or two, it was more like the whole chicken farm—dozens and dozens, a real mess."

"My goodness, I didn't notice anything when I came home," Nate remarked.

"Good, I'm glad you didn't see anything. The house looked okay to you?" Rob breathed with some relief.

"Well, I didn't know I was supposed to inspect the house. I just came inside and got in the shower."

"I think the restoration company did a really good job. But, look at the back of the house, Dad. Doesn't it look cleaner or anything?"

Nate stared at the house. "Looks the same to me."

"That's a relief. You didn't notice the house is a shade lighter, did you?"

Nate studied the house again. "I see what you're saying, now. But, it looks fine to me. So, you said they got the car, too."

"Yeah, well it was just one guy and thanks to Sharon, he has confessed. The cops charged him with a misdemeanor and he paid a fine. It's all settled."

Nate turned toward Sharon. "You had something to do with this? I can't believe that."

Sharon laughed. "Well, yes, but not the way you think."

"She's a cop, Dad."

"Oh!" Nate's eyebrows went up a notch. "A cop, you say? Well, good for you."

"Officer McGillicuddy was on duty when I called to report the vandalism. Lucky for me she came right out."

And so, my son fell in love, Nate grinned to himself, *but I don't think he knows it yet.* The Lord works in mysterious ways. "And then what happened?" Nate asked.

"Sharon investigated and did a great job for us. This is the result you see here," said Rob waving at the house, "and I'm sure you will be pleased at the large checks sitting on your desk in the house."

"What checks?"

"The check from the insurance company covering one hundred percent of the damages, and the second check from Beetle and Bailey LLC law firm covering twice the damages."

"Are you kidding me?"

"Mom and I both signed off."

Nate looked from one to the other, and took a slug of his soda. "Well, young lady, I'm impressed. Thank you."

"Well, I only did my job. Rob did the rest," she said modestly.

"You, too, son," said Nate. "Well, listen, if you two will excuse me, I have some things to do."

"Yes, sir," said Rob, standing politely with his dad.

"Nice to meet you, Sharon. I hope you can stay around for dinner," said Nate.

"Thanks, Dad, but we have other plans."

"Maybe another time," Nate turned to leave, smiling to himself.

Chapter 15 Kabandha's Test Flight

*T*uesday dawned clear and bright in Chicago. The fog and overcast skies from the previous day had cleared out. Kabandha rolled out of bed early, eager to get started.

This would be the third of dozens of tests of the new ACAS-Xu system for collision avoidance tuned to work in some currently difficult operational situations. It would allow multiple sensor inputs and be optimized for unmanned airborne systems operating on auto-pilot.

Because of that capability, the system could be programmed to take over the autopilot in manned aircraft, as well.

The first two tests of the system with two manned aircraft had been very promising. And so, this test would be conducted with six airplanes and six drones in the skies over a remote section of Lake Superior—a place which was out of the normal coverage of Ground Control. Almost no commercial airplanes used this corridor, and the military had been alerted to avoid flying certain Lake Superior airspace for the three-hour period.

The test airplanes would be guided by GPS with live pilots, except if there was an imminent threat of a mid-air collision, in which case the autopilot would take over and perform a collision avoidance maneuver. The unmanned drones would be entirely guided by autopilot, their route and destination pre-programmed into their onboard computers. Today's operation would be the first test of the system with more than two airplanes in the sky, simulating a crowded airspace such as exists over any large city in the world.

Tucked away in Kabandha's handbag was a simple thirty-dollar device easily obtained online, and frequently used by hired delivery drivers wishing to defeat their bosses tracking devices for a long enough time to take a nap. It was a GPS jamming device, intended to scramble GPS signals, in somewhat the same way that speeders used radar blocking devices to foil the traffic cops. Kabandha did not know how far out the jammer would work, but it would be fun to try.

Kabandha would be an observer on this flight, and so it was quite all right for her to take a window seat part-way back in the cabin, but not over the wing. She wanted a clear view of the sky.

Captain Mahoney was flying left seat. His voice came over the speaker system. "It's a beautiful day in Chicago, folks. Please buckle up for take-off and turn off all electronic devices." Within moments they were airborne and heading north over Lake Michigan. "Estimated time to our destination test-site is forty minutes."

Thirty-five minutes later, Kabandha could see they were over Lake Superior. Captain Mahoney announced, "We are approaching the test area. I will be deactivating our TCAS and our ADS systems, switching entirely to the ACAS-Xu. Counting down 10-9-8-7-6-5-4-3-2-1 activation.

"Hands are off, now. Relax, everybody you are now in God's hands." A few nervous chuckles tittered throughout the cabin.

Scientists and engineers strained to watch out the windows. Others watched the display screens in the cockpit. Occasionally another airplane or a drone would enter the conflicting airspace and show up on the display. "We've got one," announced the Captain. "Autopilot is now activated. Please remain buckled in your seats." Immediately the plane started to climb, while the target airplane was seen to descend. Cheering was heard throughout the plane.

To the casual observer, Kabandha was quietly watching the proceedings, almost hidden from view in her window seat. In truth she was watching the whole thing on her smart phone display. She had activated a simple app that would display all the airplanes in the vicinity that were giving off the GPS positioning signal. Anyone could do it, if they knew.

Kabandha watched for a half hour as one potential collision after another was successfully averted by the ACAS-Xu system. The captain's eyes never left the instruments, his hands hovering over the wheel, and his feet the rudders, ready to take over at an instant's notice. He hated not being in control. Let's face it, he didn't trust those eggheads with their computers and fancy doodads.

For that, Kabandha was thankful, as she was about to try her own private little experiment and she certainly wanted Captain Mahoney to be alert.

She reached into her bag and pulled out the GPS interference device. The thing was designed to work off 12 volt battery power and came equipped with a cord that plugged into a car's cigarette lighter. Every car and truck in America had one or more of these lighters. However hardly anyone used them for cigarettes, anymore. Instead they plugged in their battery powered devices, everything from cell phones to GPS gadgets, and converters which turned 12 volts into 110 AC alternating current.

Kabandha had refitted her GPS jamming device with a USB connector. By plugging the device into her computer, she hoped to run the jammer off the computer battery. She had no idea how well this would work, or whether it would work at all. She poised, with her eyes on her smart phone screen and her hand ready to insert the USB connector. She waited until her display showed a couple of unmanned drones approaching each other's air space. Now was the time.

Kabandha inhaled deeply and shoved it in. She held her breath as she watched the drones suddenly jerk downward and then spiral straight toward the water and plunge out of sight in the deepest part of Lake Superior, nestling quietly among the lost ships from earlier centuries. Other drones seemed to go wildly dizzy, first buzzing around like flies, two crashing together and shredding to bits. One lurched into the side of an airliner, and slid off toward the sea. The other two just seemed to drift off, out of control and then sank out of sight.

Kabandha had seen enough. She quickly disconnected her jamming device and hid it in the bottom of her bag. Also, she had her hand poised to turn off her smart phone if discovered watching it. The urge to watch was almost overwhelming and so she waited a couple minutes before she forced herself to turn it off and shove it into her bag. Likewise she closed her computer and put it away into its own case.

Fortunately the cool captain piloting her plane had been ready for any emergency. In seconds he had realized something was terribly wrong with the autopilot. His training kicked in and he pushed the override button on the instrument panel. Immediately he went on VFR, Visual Flight Rules. "Ladies and gentlemen please tighten your seat belts, we are going into a sharp banking turn," announced the captain. "This mission is aborted." In seconds the plane banked to the right, circled around and headed back to Chicago. No one spoke. All were shocked and astonished, except for Kabandha, who knew exactly what had happened and was elated. She hid her face and schooled her features into a solemn mask.

~~~~~

Agonizing Evaluation

Next day at work, an emergency meeting of scientists bordered on chaotic. Periods of stunned silence were interspersed with everyone shouting at once.

Kabandha feigned ignorance, and was easily ignored. In fact, she was listening carefully to the cacophony of voices, alert to any hint they could be making headway in answering the question, "What the hell happened".

The mere fact that the experiment was conducted out over the deepest part of the sea, made it impossible to recover any of the wreckage. Also, it mitigated any likelihood of interference from a ground based device. The idea that someone could have controlled the drones from the deck of a ship was deemed preposterous. There were too many drones and each one had a complex set of instructions in its computer controls, which the scientists had spent weeks inputting. How could anyone have hacked into that and inserted even more complex instructions into the software? Impossible. Besides, who would know enough and want to do it?

By late afternoon, the meeting had resulted in no conclusions, not even a hint of speculation as to what went wrong. Kabandha smiled to herself. These men had their brains up in the clouds, accustomed to thinking in such complex terms that they could not imagine a simple device could overcome their magnificent creation. Little David had defeated Goliath and they could not see the moon for the stars.

Kabandha soon realized she had made a strategic mistake. She should not have gotten carried away, taking down all six of the drones. She should have stopped at two. Now there was a danger that her company would scuttle the whole project. She realized she might have to speak up.

Gradually the scientists arranged themselves into small casual break-out groups of three to six guys, talking among themselves. Kabandha scooted her chair over to the nearest group and listened to their quiet discussion. At length the group fell silent having exhausted all ideas. In a quiet voice, Kabandha spoke for the first time.

"Well, if I may say something here..." she paused looking for assurance. Four pairs of eyes turned her way. One man nodded.

Kabandha continued, "I've been listening to all of the ideas being put forth. What I'm hearing is that no one seems to have a good handle on what may have happened."

They shrugged as if to say, "Duh."

"And so, I think we should simply conduct the experiment again, maybe on a smaller scale, and this time set it up to observe the drones better. What do you think?"

There were nods all around. "Perhaps we should put our minds to devising better ways to monitor the results."

After a period of silence, the weary men revived and began making suggestions. This was good. Kabandha knew that she would not need to sabotage the next experiment, thus allowing the project to go forward. In years to come, her knowledge could be put to use in a grand scheme to take out hundreds of planes at once.

In the meantime, she would continue to sharpen her skills, operating on a small scale around more remote airports all over the country, never in the same place twice. She would, then, begin to teach others. The increase in mid-air collisions would only give rise to a clamor to spur the ACAS-Xu project forward sooner and faster than originally planned.

Perhaps she had gone as far as she could in Chicago. It was time to move on.

~~~~~

Seattle Overnight

It was a bit unusual for Sally to take a day off in Seattle. The only time she really needed it was when she went to see her mother. At other times, she stayed overnight in the same hotel suite near the airport. This was one of those nights. She would relax, rest and either order "in" or defrost a dinner in her apartment-sized kitchen.

Sally was startled to hear her house phone chirp. It could be just a nuisance call. Perhaps the manager wanted to pay a courtesy call, making sure everything was all right.

"Hello, who's calling, please?"

"This is the desk. I have a call for you from a Mr. Bacon. Shall I put it through?"

Hmm, unknown, well that doesn't tell me anything. Usually she bypassed those calls. Still she never knew when something might happen to her mother. "Okay, I'll take it," she said.

"Hello Sally. I just wanted to tell you the bacon and eggs were great."

Sally gasped.

"I loved the brownies, too. Just call me the brownie lover, kiddo."

"B-but ..."

"Can we talk?"

"No, I'm afraid not."

"C'mon, sis, I saw Mom yesterday. We need to talk, don't you think?"

I don't like this, thought Sally. The hairs on her arms were standing up. She was frightened and dared say nothing.

"Y-you saw Mom?" she stammered.

"Yes, that shouldn't surprise you, Sally."

"I didn't know."

"Well, I'm not such a bad person. I try to get up there at least once a month, sometimes twice."

"Well, I guess she doesn't remember."

"Yeah, I know. It's sad," he said. "Well, listen, what time are you leaving in the morning? Maybe we could meet for some breakfast."

"I have to be to work early."

"Okay, I can figure that out. I'll meet you at the usual place for breakfast. Don't worry, I'll find you."

He hung up.

"Wait," said Sally. He was gone. She plunked down on the bed with the phone in her lap, her hands shaking. What just happened? Who is this guy? Was it really Mr. Brown? She couldn't be sure, as someone could have stolen the password. Did he really know about her mother, or was it just a lucky guess? Maybe her employer was testing her.

She sat back against the pillows and replayed every word that was said. He said a lot, but she didn't say anything–nothing that could give her away except to say she had to be to work early. Was that dangerous? She didn't think so. So, what should she do in the morning? Well, all she could do was get ready for work as usual, and eat breakfast here in the hotel as usual. If he was expecting her to eat at somewhere in the airport he was mistaken. What was he hinting at? She couldn't imagine. Well, she had to get some sleep. Whatever this was about, she couldn't change it.

Six AM came early after a restless night. Sally showered, dressed in her flight attendant's uniform, grabbed her shoulder bag and roll-aboard and headed for the elevator. Like most hotels of this type, a free breakfast was do-it-yourself style. Hotel guests served themselves from the food that was prepared and arranged by just one server. Guests made their own toast or waffles, and selected from sausage or bacon and scrambled eggs. Sally filled her plate from the offerings, added juice and coffee, and chose a seat at an empty table. She opened the free newspaper and quietly ate while she read. Her back was turned to a muted television set tuned to CNN news.

She paid no attention to the other people who came and went. There was plenty of space for people to spread out without speaking to each other, or making eye contact. Most of the guests were business people with their own concerns, who left you alone. And so, Sally barely noticed when someone pulled out the chair opposite her and sat at her table. By keeping her eyes down, she assumed the person would take the hint and say nothing. Instead, the man started to talk.

"Good bacon and eggs this morning, wouldn't you say?"

Sally choked on her food and raised her napkin to cover her mouth. Peeking over her napkin, she saw who it was and coughed into her napkin again to cover the startled look on her face. *And so, he must have been here in this hotel last night!*

"Excuse me," she said, and coughed again. She picked up her coffee and sipped a few times, and then she slapped her chest and let out one more little cough.

He spoke in low tones, "The first thing we must do is create a new password, one that no one else knows."

Sally nodded keeping her eyes averted.

"Have you seen mother?"

"Too personal," said Sally.

"Seattle Mariners?"

"Good."

"Okay, Seattle Mariners is my favorite team."

"We need to talk somewhere more private." Sally tried not to look around, but she felt very nervous. "Not on the phone. Not in my room." She covered her mouth and spoke into her food.

"All right, I'll rent a car and pick you up."

"No time." Sally glanced at her watch.

"Taxi?" He spoke very quietly, barely moving his mouth. "We could share."

"Okay, but not here. Go down the street. Pay with cash. Pick me up one block over. I need to make a purchase."

He raised an eyebrow.

Sally took out a pen and wrote "at Rite-Aid" on an empty sugar packet and added her cell phone number. She folded the note and slipped it into the sugar bowl, picked up her disposable dishes and put them in the waste container. Without looking at him, she grabbed her things and left.

Mr. Brown casually picked up a sugar packet and added half of it to his coffee. He palmed Sally's note without looking at it, took care of his things, picked up his case and left by the front door. He walked briskly down one block to the next hotel to get a taxicab. Once inside the cab he read Sally's note and instructed the cabbie, "I'll be going to the airport, but first I need to pick up my friend at the Rite Aid, one block over."

Sally was waiting at the curb. She slid in close to him and gave him a hug. "Hello, darling," she smiled.

"Did you get everything you needed, sweetheart?" he asked.

"No, they didn't have everything I needed," she said. "Ask the cabbie if he will drop us off at the nearest drugstore—one that is not a Rite-Aid."

"Change of plans," he told the driver. "Please drop us off at a different drug store."

"Sure," said the driver. In a few minutes he found another. "Is this okay?"

"Perfect," said Sally. "Please stop right here."

The taxi pulled up to the curb. She got out with her things. As Brownie reached to pay the driver in cash, he said, "Don't wait," and got out to join Sally.

"We won't go in here," said Sally. "Just let him drive away and then we will walk over to that bar across the street."

Soon they were seated in a darkened booth.

"We won't take the same cab again," said Sally in low tones. "We cannot be seen together like this. I am to be your contact, but it will only be on flight 1715, in first class. Is that clear?"

"Miss Millecan, I don't know what your relationship is with this lobbying firm. Can you tell me?"

"Well, I am just a part time employee. At first I was doing research for them, and now I am your contact person."

"What do you know about them?"

Sally thought a while. "Well, I really know very little. In fact that part is rather frustrating at times. But, the pay is good and I need the money."

"As far as you know is it an honest and legitimate firm, on the up and up, nothing shady?"

"Well, I certainly hope so. I mean, after all, it is a registered lobbying firm. They are strictly regulated, I understand. Aren't they?"

"Sally, I have done some checking and you seem like a very nice woman, honest as the day is long."

"Of course."

"You have passed a five-star background check and are cleared to work for the airline."

"Yes. What are you driving at Mr. B?"

"I'll be honest with you, Sally, we think you may be mixed up with the wrong people."

"That's preposterous! Who are you anyway?" She was feeling uncomfortable and looked around nervously.

Brown pulled a slim leather case out of an inside pocket and handed it to her. "Please don't let anyone see you look inside of this," he said as he handed it to her.

Sally turned it away from the room and opened it tightly to her chest. It read Harold L. Brown, Jr., Special Agent, Federal Bureau of Investigation, and included his ID number, the date, the FBI seal and the signature of the Director. Sally bit her lip, folded the case and quietly slid it across the table. Was this genuine? How could she know? It was too dark to examine it closely.

"But, I thought you were some kind of software engineer," she said. "I mean we have talked before."

"I am," he said. "In fact I am a senior scientist. But, I've been placed within the company, hoping that the bad guys would try and recruit me. It has taken years, but they finally did, thanks to you."

"Who is they?"

"We think that a terrorist organization is trying to infiltrate the airplane manufacturers and various suppliers as well as tech firms that supply the industry."

"Oh dear me, I didn't know."

"You did just fine."

"But what do I do now?" Sally was confused as well as scared.

"You keep doing what you are doing. Don't change a thing. The only difference is that now you will be taking messages back and forth from me to the group who we think are working for these terrorists. We don't know all their plans, but it has something to do with the software engineering on the new passenger series that is under development at our company. That's why they recruited me."

"I guess I need to know more," said Sally. "Some way I could check and make sure that ..."

"That I am who I say I am," said Brown, laughing. "Yes, of course, and we will take care of that when you get back to Washington. Remember the password, now?"

"Seattle Mariners."

"Good. Now there is a lot more to talk about, but you need to get going. And so, would it work for you if we had a bit of a dating arrangement, from time to time?"

"I'm not allowed to date the passengers or employees."

"Of course not. I'm thinking it would have to be during off-duty hours, and not at the airport."

"Maybe, after I know for certain who you are."

"I'll arrange that. For now, you need to hit the road."

She checked her watch. "Oh my goodness. You're right."

"I wish I could drive you."

"Let's not chance it. I'll hail a cab."

He stood and helped her on with her jacket, kissing the back of her neck. "Goodbye, darling."

She scrunched her shoulders where the moisture from his kiss tingled. "Goodbye."

~~~~~

DFW Dallas-Fort Worth International

A lone woman sat in a rental car fiddling with her smart phone. This parking lot was as close as she could get to the airport runways. She wasn't sure this would work. Maybe she would have to drive over to Love Field or the Executive Airport where she could get closer.

She watched the display on her phone for several minutes. This wasn't working. The display was so tiny it was crowded with planes. She would be guessing.

Instead she booted up her largest tablet PC computer, acquired the Automatic Dependent Surveillance System-Broadcast (ADS-B) signals and opened up the display full screen. She nodded with satisfaction—much better.

Kabandha had purchased another GPS jammer, one that would plug into her cigarette lighter. This one had an on/off switch. It cost a little more, but that was no problem. Even though you could aim it in one direction, the beam was still quite wide. There was no way, as yet, that she could zero in on just one aircraft. But, this was better than the clumsy one she used before. In fact, she had an assortment of models from different manufacturers. She intended to try them all.

Her first target was a two-engine commuter airliner. No need to go big, just yet. She waited until the plane was on approach, aimed her jammer in its direction and pushed the switch on. She held her breath as the plane glided smoothly onto the correct runway, slowed down and turned onto the taxiway. *Hmm, that didn't work.*

Next, she tried working another model on a small business jet. Still no change. Kabandha worked for an hour trying out her system with the different jammers, observing one after another of her target aircraft land safely with no disruption. Either her signal wasn't going far enough or the planes simply were not operating on GPS. She set the jammer down, leaned back and returned her eyes to idly watching the little icon airplanes on her PC display move about in the prescribed rectangular traffic pattern here over DFW.

Oh, wait a minute, what's this? Airplanes at the far end of the pattern were not making their right turn properly. They seemed to fly straight past and beyond the turn, flounder around a bit and circle before rejoining the pattern. Kabandha looked down at her jammer. Where she had dropped it caused it to aim right at that corner of the pattern. She checked the switch and saw she had left it on. She turned the switch off, this time keeping her eyes on the display. Sure enough the planes started behaving normally.

For the next half-hour she experimented with different positions, turning the jammer off and on. Clearly, the planes circling overhead were using GPS, but just as soon as that failed to work properly the pilots switched to VFR and got back on course. This was good to know, but it wasn't going to cause any collisions or crashes unless the conditions were so foggy that planes would be approaching entirely on instruments. She could wait for a long time before a day was that foggy, a rarity in Dallas. No doubt Chicago would be a better target for fog.

Kabandha turned off all her instruments and prepared to drive back to her room. She would have to give this some thought. She needed a different approach to the problem.

Kabandha knew there were some large commercial airliners that had already advanced into a next generation collision avoidance system which could automatically take over the autopilot in case of an imminent collision. She needed to find out which airliners had that capability and whether any of them flew into DFW. If not, she would move on to a coastal airport like Los Angeles, New York, or Washington DC where hundreds of transatlantic super-liners landed every day. Kabandha smiled to herself dreaming about targeting Airforce One. Wouldn't that be the coup of the ages, deserving of a place of highest honor in the annals of Islamic history?

Chapter 16 Arlington

Sally relaxed in bed with her novel, expecting a good night's sleep with no interruptions. After a glass of wine and a warm soak in the tub, she had donned her bunny-fleece pajamas and settled back into her pillows. She sighed deeply and opened her novel. It had been so long that she barely remembered the plot. Fortunately the description, cover and the table of contents gave her some clues. She found her book-mark and started reading the first paragraph. Ah, yes, now she remembered. Here was the handsome cowboy hero about to pick up the phone and call his girlfriend.

Just then Sally's cell phone chirped. For a second she wasn't sure if it was her imagination. It chirped again. *Darn it.* She picked up the phone from her bedside table. This had better not be Edward or someone from Vancouver. The display read "unknown caller." *Fiddlesticks!*

"Hello, who's calling?" she demanded.

"Hello Sally, it's the Seattle Mariners calling."

"What the heck are they calling about?"

"You sound like you don't love us anymore."

"Oh, okay, you know darn well, I love the Seattle Mariners."

"Then we agree," said Brown, "I'll be brief, sweetie, how about lunch tomorrow?"

"I expect to eat lunch, yes."

"Good, be downstairs by 11:30, okay?"

"Yup," Sally agreed, clicked her phone off and set it back on the table, none too softly.

Sighing, she picked up her book and read the same paragraph again.

~~~~~

Lunch with Brownie

"Where are we going?" asked Sally as Harold Brown Jr. turned onto the DC Beltway.

"Headquarters," he answered.

"What?"

"You'll see," he said grinning at her.

Fifteen minutes later, Brown exited onto Pennsylvania Avenue, drove just past a large plain brown building, seven stories high and turned right twice. He entered an underground ramp, halting at the guard post. Lowering the window he handed the guard the same slim brown leather ID she had seen in Seattle. The armed guard examined it carefully, compared the photo with Harold Brown, checked his roster and handed back the ID wallet. "May I see your ID, Miss?" he inquired. Sally began fishing in her purse.

"She's with me," said Brown, as he held out his hand for her ID. Sally gave him her driver's license, which he passed to the guard who gave her the same inspection routine. Giving it back, he handed Brown a clip board. "Please sign in here," he said. Brown scribbled his signature and and passed it to Sally. "Sign this, please," he stated.

As they were waved through, Brown added, "Hang on to that ID, honey, you'll be needing it. And, by the way, so long as we are dating like this, you may call me Hal, or Hey You, or whatever feels good at the time." He laughed and expertly steered down a long ramp to the sub-basement where he found a parking spot. "Are you hungry?" he asked.

"Yes, I am, Hal," Sally answered, feeling somewhat relieved that Hal seemed to be the genuine article, at least so far. She rather doubted that a terrorist could get inside this building. Well, maybe not. Who knows where there were? They certainly seemed to be everywhere–the Air Force, Army and serving as guards in a variety of venues. She would withhold judgement, just a tiny bit before concluding that Hal was who he said he was.

Hal glanced at his watch. "I think we have time to visit the cafeteria, before our appointment. But, first I want to take just a second and show you the courtyard. It's really nice."

He led her past a crowded Starbucks into an open courtyard, landscaped with flowers and low shrubbery. Walkways meandered through the courtyard where groupings of small tables and chairs were situated under flowering trees. Others were colorful umbrella tables. Employees were gathered around the tables, enjoying their break, with coffee and popped corn from the free kettlecorn dispensers.

"Isn't this something to see," asked Hal, "right here in downtown Washington?"

Back inside, they took the elevator up to the cafeteria level. It was very nice, but more like a typical cafeteria with all manner of salads, and a center island with a huge variety of hot and cold dishes. To one side was a deli where one could get hamburgers, pizza and sandwiches to order. Another area displayed a vast number of desserts. A large seating area contained different sized tables with seating for one to six people. Booths were along one wall, and another area had stools at a soft drink bar.

Hal and Sally made their selections and carried their trays through open doors to a smaller outdoor covered rooftop patio area.

After they took their places she realized that a lot of fashionably dressed women and others in civilian attire worked here. In fact, looking around she didn't see a single tough guy. Most were like Hal, middle aged, middle sized, average types, dressed like any other business man.

They ate in silence, enjoying the ambiance of mingled voices, fragrances and bird calls with very little traffic noise penetrating from the outside world.

In fact, sitting there, Sally realized there were no airplanes flying overhead. This was a restricted air space. If any hapless Cessna pilot strayed near the seat of power, a contingent of military jets politely escorted him to a nearby base where he would pay dearly for his transgression—probably a fine and several hours of interrogation before he was sent on his way, older and wiser.

"Well, our appointment is at one. Let's wrap this up," Hal suggested.

Sally quickly finished her salad and downed the last of her iced tea. They picked up their trays and placed everything in the designated receptacles. "Over this way," said Hal and he led her to another corridor where the rest rooms were located. "I'll meet you right here, okay?" asked Hal.

"Sure, fine," Sally agreed.

An elevator whisked them to the seventh floor, opening to yet another corridor. Hal escorted Sally to the very end where an imposing door said Director Christopher A. Wray. "We'll just duck in here for a brief minute. He's a busy guy." He knocked lightly and opened the door. A man looked up from the reception desk. Hal showed their IDs. "We're here to see the director for a moment."

"I'll let him know you are here. Please sign in, both of you." He indicated a clip board on the corner of his desk as he turned to buzz the director. "Special Agent Harold Brown, Jr. and Miss Sally Millecan to see you, sir." To Hal and Sally he said, "Please have a seat."

Hal took Sally's hand and led her over to a seating arrangement where they sat down. "Is this really the director's office?" Sally whispered. "I don't believe this."

"Hello, Hal," came a jovial voice, as footsteps sounded.

Hal immediately stood. "Director Wray," he took the extended hand.

"Oh come now, Hal. It's still Chris to you," said a slim man, with brown hair and blue eyes, a square jaw and crooked smile.

"Director Wray... I mean Chris... I'd like to present Miss Sally Millecan."

"Well, hello there, Sally," he said.

"Director Wray," said Sally in awe.

"How nice of you to bring Miss Millecan here to meet me, Hal."

"Thank you, sir. We just stopped in for a minute. Sally and I are on our way over to the Counter-Terrorism Division."

"Excellent, Hal. Good luck with that. You are doing a great job. We appreciate your work. You, too, Sally."

"Thank you, Chris," said Hal.

"Thank you, Director Wray," said Sally.

Hal took her hand and they turned to leave.

Moving down the hall, Hal leaned over to whisper in her ear, "Are you convinced yet?"

Sally blushed.

"Come with me, honey, there's one more person I want you to meet," he said.

"I don't suppose you could give me a clue," she retorted.

"Sure, I can. This person is really my boss, or maybe my boss's boss."

"Didn't I just meet your boss's boss?"

"Naw, that was my boss's boss's boss."

"Oh my! You are way down the line, aren't you?"

"Not so. Just ask anyone and they'll tell you that those bosses are just here to serve us."

"Umm, yeah, sure."

"Here we are," Hal paused in front of another door, National Security Branch. Executive Assistant Director, Caroline Douglas. With one finger he underlined the last line.

"A woman?" Sally asked.

Hal grinned. "Forty years ago there were no women agents. Now look. They've taken over."

"Well, good for her."

"Yup. Let's go in." Hal opened the door. There was another reception desk and another man greeting them. Sally was getting the hang of it. She walked up to the desk and offered her ID, picked up the pen and signed in.

"Thank you, Miss Millecan," said the man.

"We're here to see Ms. Douglas," said Hal.

"Yes sir, she's expecting you. Go right in."

"This way," said Hal, taking her hand. They walked down a wide corridor flanked on either side with offices, until they reached a large office suite with another reception desk. "She's on the phone with the director. It will be a few minutes. Can I get you something?" asked the assistant.

"Nothing for me, thank you," said Sally.

"No thanks," said Hal. "We'll wait right over here." He motioned for Sally to sit. It was only slightly smaller and less plush than the director's waiting area.

They waited. Sally tried not to fidget with her hands, but it was almost impossible, she was so nervous wondering if they were going to arrest her at any moment, for something– anything–she had no idea what. Did they need a reason?

It seemed like forever, but eventually Ms. Douglas came out of her room and greeted them with hand extended. "Hello Sally, I'm so happy you are here. And Hal, where did you find this brilliant woman?"

Hal made the introductions, "Executive Assistant Director Douglas, may I present Miss Sally Millecan, Flight Attendant with Alaska Airlines and Virgin America Airlines. Sally, meet the head of the FBI's counter-terrorism division, my boss's boss."

"How do you do, Director Douglas," said Sally formally. She wiped her sweaty palm before she took the director's offered hand.

"Nonsense, please call me Carrie. I'm delighted to have you here, my dear. Please come in. I'll get you a drink."

"No thank you, I'm good," said Sally.

"Not at all, I insist. We'll have a drink. What time is it anyway, Hal?"

"Um, I think it's five o'clock somewhere," Hal hesitated.

"Good, now Hal, you just sit right there, while I serve," said Douglas. She bent over, opening a little refrigerator. "We have rum and coke, lite beer, tomato juice and flavored water."

"Water will be fine, thank you, Director Douglas," said Sally, still standing.

"No, Sally, it's Carrie. Get it? Care...eee."

"Carrie," said Sally, trying to smile.

"Very good," Caroline enthused. "You're going to fit right in."

"Fit in?" asked Sally in some bewilderment.

Caroline gazed solemnly at Hal, "You haven't told her?"

Hal shook his head, looking guilty.

"In that case, mister, all you get is the water. Sally and I will split a beer." She took one beer and poured a little into two pretty glasses. Handing one to Sally, she said, "Let's drink to a world without men. What do you say?"

Finally Sally could laugh, "Hear, hear," she said, taking the exquisite crystal stemware in her hand. Two glasses clinked delicately and were tipped for a sip. In turn, four eyes scowled at Hal. "All right, what didn't he tell me?" inquired Sally.

"Forget him," said Caroline, as she pulled Sally aside. "Sit over here with me. Bring your beer." She filled their glasses.

"All right, here's the scoop," she began. "It's very simple. We want you to work for us."

Sally gasped and looked at first one, then the other. "What!"

"Whatever they are paying you, we'll pay you double."

"Huh?" Suddenly Sally needed the beer.

"Don't worry, you can keep their salary, too." Caroline picked up the bottle and topped off Sally's glass.

Sally just stared at them, open-mouthed.

Caroline scowled at Hal again. "You should have told her, Brownie. The poor girl is in shock." She chuckled.

~~~~~

DC Snooper

Outside Andrews Air Force base, Kabandha tried working her little system. Fighter jets and large cargo airplanes came and went. She could see them on her display, but none of them seemed to be affected by her jammer. For a couple of hours she tried various configurations.

Giving up in frustration, she started up the rental car. She had driven all the way from Dallas, not wanting to leave traces of her movements. The little jammer came in handy for that purpose. She kept it on, so that Avis couldn't track her car. No telling what receivers she was jamming in the process. Kabandha shrugged that off as collateral damage. Stuff happens.

Kabandha had to turn off her jammer for a few minutes so she could use her onboard GPS to find her way to Dulles International Airport. Perhaps it might be a more accessible target. Dulles was huge with multiple runways and parking lots. She drove around the labyrinth of roads several times before she figured it out.

By now she was hungry and had a full bladder. She chose a parking lot that was not too crowded and moved off into a corner to take care of her bodily functions and needs. With a full belly, having driven many hours without sleep, Kabandha was ready for a nap. But, this mission was too important to waste time sleeping. Kabandha took a pep pill out of her bag and swallowed it with a sip of an energy drink.

She fought to stay awake until the caffeine kicked in. She needed enough time to make this one last test. If it didn't work she would have to come up with another system. Her eyelids fluttered as her mind wandered off, thinking ahead to the possible use of a software defined radio, sleepily conjuring up a sequence of false commands that could be inputted into a superliner's collision avoidance system. There were any number of ways she could envision ruining a pilot's day. Perhaps a bevy of false airplanes could suddenly show up on the instrument panel display. Kabandha chuckled to herself. The poor pilot wouldn't know which one to avoid. Or, she could have the onboard warning voice rapidly shout, "Pull up, descend, pull up, descend," over and over.

Suddenly Kabandha woke up, chiding herself when she realized she had been dreaming. Then again, maybe it wasn't just a dream. Could it be the ancestors were sending her a message? *Hmm, software defined radio, that might work. Only problem is that the radio would have to be onboard the plane.* This would be a suicide mission for the operator. Not that that would be too much to pay, but there weren't enough skilled technicians in their ranks. Could we afford to lose one? *Certainly not me*, she thought. *Okay, let's get back to business, here.*

Kabandha shook her head to clear it and swallowed some more of her energy drink. She went about setting up her first test, booting up her laptop, activating the display and aiming her jammer at the closest area of the holding pattern. She was in luck. Airplanes were circling almost directly overhead, each at a separate altitude, stacked up waiting for the cleared-to-land order. Kabandha had to back the car and move it around a bit so that she would have a clear shot with her jammer. This was perfect. She aimed her jammer at the sky and turned it on.

Eyes glued to her display, fingers crossed, she held her breath. A few seconds passed and then the first plane missed its turn, and then the second and a third. Eureka! Success!

Hastily, Kabandha switched off the jammer, lest she arouse suspicion. Elated, she would wait until all these planes had recovered and landed safely before she dared try the system again.

She waited a full hour, and then tried it again on only two airplanes this time, waited again and tried it on just one airplane. Each time it worked flawlessly. Kabandha now knew she had invented the perfect terrorism tool. *Thank you, Allah.* It was cheap, simple and teachable. She could train a hundred brothers to operate as a team, at multiple airports at once. By simultaneously operating cheap drones, laser beams and GPS jammers, they could send an unsuspecting airliner directly into a drone equipped with explosives. Multiple accidents all over the country would overwhelm systems and send the country into chaos. Perhaps some brothers or sisters would be lost. It mattered not. Those few minions would be expendable for the cause. In the meantime, higher powers would be at work, taking advantage of the chaos to launch even more deadly attacks.

Kabandha packed up her things and drove away. She would allow herself to sleep, at last. Tomorrow she would visit headquarters, report her findings, and receive the well-earned plaudits of the leaders.

~~~~~

Men Work from Sun to Sun

Feeling relaxed and rested, Nate stretched and opened one eye to check the clock. 5:00 AM. And then he remembered: Oh yeah, I have to catch a flight at seven. He rolled over on his side and peeked at Nan, wondering if there was any chance she might be awake. If so, he had time for a "quickie" before he had to leave. Watching the bedclothes covering her gently rise and fall, he concluded she was either fast asleep or doing a good job of play possum. Oh well, he sighed and eased out of bed. He loved her enough to let her rest.

Today's flight was a long one in three segments. He would fly from here to the hub airport, and then catch a long flight to Montreal, continuing to Washington DC. It was unusual to fly into Canada where he had no jurisdiction. But cooperation between the two countries was complete and long-standing. Nate had never had any problems, in that regard. Terrorists knew no boundaries and so all flights had to be covered.

Tonight he would bed down in DC and tomorrow he would check in with his boss at FAMS, the Federal Air Marshal Service. FAMS was a part of the TSA—Transportation Security Administration—which was just one little part of that huge conglomerate, the Department of Homeland Security (DHS). Mind you, even that was under the FBI. No, wait a minute, FBI was under the Justice Department. How on earth they kept track of each other was a mystery to Nate. Sometimes he wondered whether they knew he existed. Do you suppose that if he died, the paychecks would keep coming? He chuckled at the thought.

~~~~~

They Quarrel

"I'm sorry, Sally," Hal pleaded. "I know it was unfair. But ..."

"No buts," Sally interrupted. "How could you?" she stormed.

"I'm sorry, really I am. I had no right. But, please hear me out."

They were seated outside the FBI building in Hal's car.

"Look Mr. Br–whoever you are–we shouldn't even be talking here and you know it." Her voice was on the edge of hysteria.

"You want to go back inside?"

"Are you kidding me? Back inside that den of thieves?"

"I get it, you don't want to go back," said Hal sadly.

"You got one thing right."

"Well, maybe the best thing is just to drive."

"How do I know you aren't wearing a wire or running some kind of secret recording device?"

"Um, I guess you don't."

Sally was silent. She dug a handful of tissues out of her purse, started dabbing her eyes and staring out the window.

"Well, what are you going to do?" Hal asked hesitantly. He hated it when women cried.

"I don't know. I just don't know." She threw up her hands and cried in earnest.

"Uh, don't cry, Sally," he said completely at a loss. "Uh, maybe ... maybe you just have to trust me."

Sally looked at him in astonishment, "Trust you?" She bawled in earnest.

I guess I said the wrong thing, thought Hal.

"Well, okay, I-I'll just drive you home," he said, disconsolately, and started the car.

Pulling up in front of her apartment building, Hal put the car in "Park" with the engine running.

He laid his arm over the back of her seat and looked earnestly into her face. "Sally, I'm sorry, but I think we need to talk. Can I come in? Please."

Sally gave him her best disgusted look, picked up her handbag, threw the strap over her shoulder, open her door and flounced out with a determined stride and her chin in the air.

Hal called after her, "I'll text you in the morning."

~~~~~

Trapped

Tucked into her bed, Sally thought it through. It was clear. They had her. The FBI didn't have to spell it out. She was working for terrorists. Either she cooperated with the FBI or they would make sure she was ruined. Her reputation, her clearance, her job–all gone, at the very least. At the worst, prison for treason. *Oh my God! They want me to be a spy, a double agent.* She cried some more.

Hal was one of them! And she was starting to like him–a low-down liar! *Oh my God!* She cried harder, feeling like a bird in a trap. Oh how she wished she had a dad she could call for help, or a mother who would listen to her, or could listen to her. She was alone, an orphan. She didn't have friends, really, just people she saw at work and customers of the airlines. Look where that got her. *Oh my God,* she moaned.

Well, that's absolutely right, God is all I have. Sally got out of bed and down on her knees with tears on her face and hands clasped heavenward on the bed. "Father in Heaven," she began, "I need you, now. You know my troubles and you know everyone's hearts. I pray that you will guide and direct me into the right path and the right decision, and that you will protect me." She waited.

A feeling of peace settled around her like a warm blanket. "Thank you, God, Amen," she finished, arose from her knees and got back into bed. Within minutes she was asleep.

Chapter 17 As Fate Would Have It

Kabandha

She woke early too excited to sleep. Today would be a triumphant day for her. Kabandha would be going downtown to meet the leaders for the first time in her life. After her presentation she expected to be the toast of the entire organization.

Kabandha had always known she was gifted. By the time she was eight years old, she could out-think her siblings and had mastered two languages. In her early teens she often taught her parents, who were hard-working, wholesome simple believers, but uneducated. She became the bookkeeper for the family and often the spokesperson. Throughout her school years she advanced quickly and soon learned she was smarter than her teachers. Having none other with whom to compare, she learned that she was also the smartest person in her small home town in rural Minnesota. She kept this knowledge to herself, not realizing what it meant until she attended the nearby junior college and continued to ace all her courses, which was later confirmed when she graduated from the university summa-cum-laude. It wasn't until she reached graduate school that she had competition and began to meet people who were intellectual equals. What a relief it was to discover she was not alone in the world! It was there that Kabandha was introduced to her life's work, ji-had, a cause larger than herself, worthy of her talents—her mission.

~~~~~

Nate

It was morning in DC. Nate had slept well. He wasn't scheduled downtown until mid-morning, and so he took his time rousting about. He never got used to the changing time zones, different each night. He shuffled into the bathroom and started the small coffee-maker. While it perked he used the urinal. Studying his face in the mirror he noticed a few more gray hairs on the sides—too many to count. Didn't they say it made a man look distinguished? He ran the palm of his hand over his five o'clock shadow. Should he shave it off clean in honor of his visit with the boss today? *Naw, why bother?* He felt more comfortable this way. Nan told him it looked sexy. Should he call her? *No, she would still be asleep.*

Propped up in bed, with his first cup of morning brew, Nate opened his email account and sent her a good morning message. "Good morning, darling. In DC this morning. Should be a nice day. Nothing much happening. Anything you want me to pick up in the big city? Love you lots, Nate"

~~~~~

Edward

Edward fought for a place at the table and a decent share of the food. With six siblings crowded around it was always first-come-first-served, and the food vanished in a hurry. He was the second oldest in the family and expected to earn his keep. Most of his salary went to support the family. The firstborn son, George, had left home and was somewhere in Chicago, working hard at a job, so far as Edward knew. George never sent any money home. In fact, Edward resented that his mother frequently sent some of his hard-earned money to George. She was secretive about that, but he knew. There was never enough, what with his father driving a cab and his mother doing odd jobs for rich Americans. That was why Edward had taken this job with the lobbying firm. It was a steady paycheck and a worthy cause, so far as he knew. He was careful not to ask questions. Today he would report for work at the usual time.

~~~~~

Sally

Sally Millecan opened one eye. Where was she? Immediately she recognized her own bedroom in Arlington. Feeling safe, she closed the eye and pulled up the covers for another forty winks. In a few minutes her mind started to work. Thinking back on yesterday's events, she smiled slightly when she thought of Caroline Douglas, a brilliant and wildly successful woman, heading an organization of thousands of employees, and much to be admired. Sally realized, now that the whole scene, yesterday, was Carrie's ingenious attempt to put her at ease. It worked. This was someone she could work with and work for. Sally doubted that very many employees of Homeland Security referred to Ms. Douglas as Carrie. Sally almost laughed aloud.

Sally remembered her crying jag of yesterday. Yes, it was true, she was caught in a situation. She would have to forgive Hal, and accept his lifeline, so far as that went. Crying helped, but so did prayer. Sally lifted up another prayer, asking for protection. She was ready to face the day and the unknown, trusting no one else but God to pull her through.

~~~~~

Hal

Not much he could do about yesterday but go with the flow. He regretted it had been necessary to deceive Sally. She would never have agreed to serve as a double agent voluntarily. She was sucked into the vortex. Too bad he had to do what he had to do, because he was beginning to like her. Normally he preferred petite blond women who were short and sweet. Sally could almost look him in the eye when she wore heels. And he wasn't really sure what color hair she had, some kind of medium brown. Those brown eyes, though, oh my, he was hypnotized by her eyes. He was more than half-way serious when he kidded her about dating.

Well, enough of this kind of thinking. He had to get going and face the music. Maybe Sally would have mellowed by this morning.

Hal grabbed his phone and texted her a message. "Will pick you up at eight. Be ready."

~~~~~

Caroline

The FBI never really slept. This building was online 24/7. Caroline Douglas, head of the FBI's huge National Security Branch, was in early dealing with a multitude of items that came in overnight. "Set up a meeting for eight o'clock," she instructed John, her personal executive assistant. "I want to see Shapiro, Bell and Mason and whomever they can grab to bring along." These men were heads of FBI's counter-terrorism, the Transportation Security Administration (TSA) and the Federal Air Marshal Service (FAMS), respectively. "You need to sit-in on the meeting, too, John."

Later they gathered around a table in the conference room.

"I believe we are nearing the time when we can close in on this terrorism cell operating out of DC," Douglas began. "We've had a breakthrough, I think."

"And that would be?" asked Mason, head of the Federal Air Marshals.

"You tell him," said Douglas to Shipiro, head of the FBI's counter-terrorism unit.

"We have had rumors that they have made attempts to place spies in the airplane industry, and so we have personnel working on that angle. Special Agent Harold Brown Jr. has his degree in software science, and so we assigned him to the task of... well... working for one of the largest suppliers to airplane manufacturing companies, acting as bait. It was a long shot, but we hoped they would approach him and so he made himself available in various ways. Brown is one of our best. Last week he lucked out and they hired him to infiltrate and sabotage the software design area as their agent."

"How on earth could he do that?" John was incredulous thinking of the redundancy in every airplane part and the multiple inspections that must be past.

"Well, I don't understand this myself," said Shapiro, "but apparently they think that tiny malicious fake lines of code could be added into the millions of lines of code that will control the new traffic control guidance system that is due to come on line in the next decade. These spy codes, we call them, would look like normal code and would be buried in the system awaiting activation years later."

"I still don't get it."

"Neither do I," answered Shapiro, "but I'm sure TSA is in charge of the development. Bell could explain it better than I can. Apparently there will be a collision avoidance system installed in every airplane that will take over in case of a close call. Is that right, Bell?"

"Keep going," said Bell, "I'm interested in learning what you know."

"Um, well," Shapiro continued, "I'm out of my depth here, but one thing the spy code could do when activated is misdirect two airplanes so they would crash, instead of avoiding each other."

"And you've got this Harold somebody who can actually write this code?" asked Bell, clearly doubting it.

"Not necessarily. But, we are pretty sure he can fake it. Remember the terrorists have their experts, too, and they would be helping. Really, we are excited that Brown has provided us with one of the missing links we needed, a link to the central terrorist organization."

"What organization? Who are they?" asked Bell, head of the TSA—Transportation Security Administration's airport security unit.

"It's a pseudo-lobbying firm we've had our eye on for some time," answered the FBI's man.

"Oh, yeah?" asked Bell. "Al Qaeda?"

"We don't know that. It could be just a domestic group. But, of course, they're all linked together by the same ideology—jihad," said FBI's Shapiro. "We think that their goal is to cause wide-scale disruption by bringing down domestic airliners using high tech means."

TSA's Bell drew himself up and added, importantly, "We all know, of course, airport security has completely thwarted any efforts to get a bomb on board," he couldn't resist bragging a bit, tooting his own horn.

"Right, Bell," said Caroline Douglas, "So far, so good. But, you can never relax. You must stay ahead of them," she added, bringing him up short. "We're all in this together."

"Exactly," Bell agreed, having been chastised by the boss.

"And this missing link, who is it?" asked John who had said very little, so far.

"The very woman you met yesterday, John, the nice-looking young woman who came in with Hal Brown," Douglas answered.

"Didn't I see her crying when they left?" asked John.

"I wouldn't be surprised," said Douglas. "She was pretty shaken up."

"What did you do to her?" accused Mason, the senior member of the group and only one who dared ask that question. Mason had been the head of the Federal Air Marshal service for more years than anyone could count.

Caroline assumed an innocent look, "Who me? Nothing at all. Must have been Hal."

"Yeah sure," Shapiro interjected. "Not my man, no way."

"Perhaps it was the reality of the situation," suggested Douglas. "She seemed to have no idea how or with whom she had gotten entangled. We'll just have to wait and see how that plays out. For now, she is reluctantly working for us, but her attitude will improve, we hope. Her background checks out beautifully, so no problem there. We plan to follow her to her contact who will lead us to the lobbying firm."

"Who is this woman?" asked Bell.

"You do not need to know. We'll just call her Sally."

"And this Sally works for one of us?" Bell was incredulous, and gazed around the table suspiciously.

"You, actually," Caroline laughed and pointed a finger at Bell, "in her day job."

Bell coughed and took a sip of water.

Everyone else studied their hands and schooled their faces. Bell had a bit of a reputation as a pompous ass who enjoyed putting the women under him in their places.

"How much time do we have?" asked Bell, changing the subject.

Caroline looked around. "We need to take time to build our case, wouldn't you say?" Everyone nodded except Mason. He shook his head.

"You don't agree?" asked Caroline of Mason.

"Well, they could be closer than we think."

"Why is that?"

"They haven't been relying entirely on the airplane industry connection. They may be exploring more than one means to bring down a plane."

"I suppose so, but we know that the TSA has been successful in upgrading their inspections," Caroline decided to hand Bell a bone. "So what else is there?"

"Well ... we've been following a sub-group out of Chicago," Mason explained. "One of our undercover Air Marshals stopped a chap who was threatening a flight attendant with a smuggled six-inch switchblade," said Mason, trying not to look at Bell.

Caroline had no such qualms. Drilling Bell with her practiced glare, she inquired, "And how did this chap manage to get a weapon on board a domestic airliner?" She already knew, but wanted it to be said aloud.

"This knife was made of a top-secret material that will pass through security," said Mason in level tones.

"Impossible!" sputtered Bell.

There was a stunned silence.

"Go on," Caroline invited.

"It's a bit of a long story," Mason offered.

"Summarize," said Douglas, "just give us the important points."

"Okay, well, our agent, Nate Goodrich, was able to thwart the attempt, and alert our local office. The man was arrested, let go, and later murdered by another member of the cell. We shot that guy. Were able to question him just a little before he died. All we got was the name of his cell leader, a woman named Kabandha. We hypothesized that the cell was connected with a larger terrorist group. I'm wondering now, whether it could be the one here in DC.

"Fortunately a neighbor had noticed suspicious activity and called in a tip. Even so, the woman named Kabandha managed to slip away. Turns out she was a top scientist working at a small firm which is designing and testing a totally new air traffic control guidance system which is due to come out in a few years. I'm sure that Bell can fill us in on that." He smiled at Bell. "In the meantime we assigned an agent to locating and following the woman. She left Chicago and turned up in Dallas in a rental car parked outside DFW. We lost track of her for a full day until a day ago when her rental car's GPS gave off a brief signal."

"Where did the signal come from?"

"It was a strange thing," said Mason. "Right here is DC, the car was driving from Andrews to Dulles where it parked in a lot. And then we lost contact."

"Oh my God!" Bell exclaimed. "That all adds up."

"What adds up?" Douglas demanded.

"Well, we've had a few guidance problems reported from airliners."

"Why don't I know about this?" her voice rose.

"W-we're investigating," said Bell, color creeping up his neck.

"And just exactly how many pilots from how many airliners reported these guidance problems?"

"There were two at once at Dallas-Fort Worth, and then an hour later, one more. And then the same thing happened at Dulles a whole day later. In this case three, then two a while later, and finally just one airliner."

"What sort of guidance problems?"

"All they said was that the guidance system suddenly cut out when they were scheduled to make a turn in the traffic pattern and they returned to the intended flight path using VFR—Visual Flight Rules. And then it seemed to come back on."

"No doubt you have the exact time of these incidents."

"Yes, of course," he had recovered his attitude, "I have it right here." He handed her a page.

She looked at the printout and then passed it to Mason, who examined the paper. "Could just be a coincidence," said Mason, "but it appears the timing coincides with our terrorist's visits to those airports." He handed the paper back to Bell.

"Do we have a description of this woman?" asked Douglas.

"We're working on that right now," said Mason. "We know her place of employment in Chicago and are hoping to get a picture from her personnel records. If not that, at least her full name and a driver's license picture."

"Very good," said Caroline. "Hurry that, and we'll meet back here at nine o'clock. Good morning, gentlemen." She stood and left the room, moving back to her office.

The men continued to confer.

"Do you have the name of the company she worked for in Chicago?" asked Bell. "You said they were designing and testing air guidance systems for the FAA."

"Yeah, I did. I'll have to look it up," said Mason. "Ring any bells with you, Mr. Bell? Sorry, bad pun."

"It sure does. We need to know if it's the same company who've reported some testing problems. If so I need to talk to them immediately. I have a really bad feeling about this."

"Give me just a minute, while I call my office," said Mason.

Mason listened for a minute and then wrote a name on a slip of paper. "Thank you," he said and clicked off, shoving the paper over to Bell.

Bell glanced at the paper, "Oh my God in Heaven." He gasped, "She works for the very same outfit that is testing our new ACAS guidance system. They reported a loss of six unmanned drones on their third round of tests and only two on their fourth round. We thought that was progress. I'll have to call their CEO. We need to know whether this Kabandha has anything to do with the development. Holy Cow! What if?"

"What if what?" asked Shapiro.

"What if she is working for the terrorists at the same time she is designing and programing our new guidance system?"

"Oh my God!" said Shapiro.

"Well, I'll make those calls and see you back here at nine," said Bell, grabbing his briefcase and hurrying out the door.

Shapiro and Mason looked at each other.

"Wow," said Shapiro.

"Yeah," said Mason. "I'm thinking I'd better have all my people on board at nine o'clock."

"We're thinking the same thing," said Shapiro. "I'll see if I can round up Hal Brown and Sally what's-her-name, assuming she hasn't flown the coop."

"We're in luck. The Air Marshal who brought down the Chicago group is due in today. I'll bring him. I may have the agent who was following Kabandha, too. I'll see."

The both hurried out.

Chapter 18 A Little After Nine AM

T he little group had expanded. In addition to Caroline Douglas and her exec. assistant John, FBI's Shapiro had brought Harold Brown Jr. and Sally, and TSA's Bell had brought photographs of Kabandha Ghana, along with her ID, address and description. Everyone gathered around the table, taking their seats, and began to examine the documents.

Caroline Douglas opened the meeting, "Thank you for coming. I know you had to hurry. We are here to discuss the terrorist group we refer to as the Lobby Group. Since we broke up a half hour ago, more information has come out regarding this Kabandha Ghana. I believe that Bell has something to say."

"Thank you, Ms. Douglas."

"Call me Caroline, please."

"Yes, well, Caroline, after you left the room we discovered a possible connection between this Kabandha person and the guidance system breakdowns that have been reported. And so, I called our supplier in Chicago, and confirmed that Kabandha has been one of the chief software engineers on the design team. Also, she was present when the prototype of the new ACAS-Xu guidance system was field tested over Lake Superior. At that time six drones were lost because of failure in the system. On the next test, over land, this time, Kabandha was also present. Two drones were lost on that test. Those drones were recovered. At this point they have not been able to find the cause of the failure. I asked the CEO if it was possible that an external source could have disrupted the guidance system. He said that the test area was too remote. Any type of interference would have to be close, within a few miles."

"Maybe this is a dumb question," said John, "but could interference have come from an airplane or a nearby boat?"

"Not dumb at all. In fact that is the big question. It seems that if interference of some sort caused the failures, it had to come from one of the aircraft already in the test, or from a nearby boat. The no-fly zone was quite large.

"In addition to these facts, we also learned that Kabandha happened to be in two different airports at the exact time as three incidents of guidance failure have been reported in the last few days."

Caroline summed it up, "So now we know of seven separate incidents of guidance failure when Kabandha was present. What more do we need to know?"

"Is she a terrorist?"

"What are her plans or plots or motives?"

"Who is she connected with?"

"That's good," said Caroline. "What else?"

Everyone thought.

"What else?" she repeated.

"How close are they?" said a small voice.

"That's exactly right, Sally. You nailed it. Okay folks how much time do we have?"

The room was silent. No one knew the answer.

Caroline glanced at her watch as if to make the point. Time was passing.

Just then. Mason, the head of the Federal Air Marshal service walked in, with another gentleman. They found two places at the end.

"Welcome to our group discussion," said Caroline. "You're late," she scowled.

"I apologize for disrupting your discussion, Ms. Douglas and distinguished people," said Mason with a slight tip of his head.

She waved off his apology. "Never mind that, just please introduce your guest," she said. "We need to move on."

"I tried to get the agent who has been following Kabandha. That's why we were late. Maybe he will be in later.

"My other guest today is one of our very best Federal Air Marshals, the hero of the take-down of terrorist George F. George, and many others, Mr. Nate Goodrich."

There was polite applause.

"Thank you Mr. Goodrich for your service," said Caroline. "You were instrumental in exposing the Chicago cell, headed by an unidentified woman."

Nate acknowledge it by a nod of his head.

"We have since identified that woman, Mr. Goodrich, and have followed her here to Washington DC. The woman, Kabandha Ghana is a brilliant scientist and has her doctorate in Computer Software Science. We suspect she has discovered a system to interfere with the guidance systems of aircraft and has successfully tried it out in at least seven different instances.

"We also know of a lobbying firm in DC which we suspect is working undercover as a terrorist organization dedicated to taking down an American domestic flight, or many flights. What we don't know, is whether Kabandha is part of that organization. If so, she could be in DC to report her findings and set up a plot."

Caroline paused. "Here is her picture and description. Have you ever seen her, Mr. Goodrich?" Nate shook his head.

"I have more photos to pass around," said Shapiro. He started handing out photos one by one. People looked at them and passed them on. "This is a lineup of suspects mixed in with employees and models. The suspects are photos we've obtained of the lobbyist organization that may, or may not, be involved in working for terrorists. Bear in mind, we have yet to prove anything against them." The pictures were going around the table. "Please speak up if any of these faces look familiar to you."

John started laughing and quickly passed a picture on.

"John?" asked Caroline. "What did you see?"

He shook his head.

"C'mon John." Caroline urged.

"Well, I hesitate to say as I'm pretty sure it is against company policy."

"I see."

"It's just that that girl works here. I've dated her."

Everyone laughed, except Caroline. "Then, I assume you can vouch for her character."

"Yes, ma'am," said John sheepishly.

"Please remove that photo from the lot," said Caroline.

Just then, Sally gasped, holding a picture. Her hand came to her mouth. "That's Edward!"

"May I see that?" asked Shapiro. Sally handed it over.

"Can you say more about Edward?" asked Caroline, gently.

"Edward is my contact ... well, my main contact. There is also a teen age girl, but so far, I haven't seen her picture."

"Thank you Sally. That could be a really important clue. Let's keep the pictures moving," said Caroline.

No others were recognized.

"Well, we have a start," said Caroline, tapping a manicured fingernail on a picture. "Shapiro, can you share with us just which of these pictures are your suspects?"

"Yes, I can do that." He sorted out a half dozen, plus the shot of Edward. "These are all people we have identified as being part of the lobbying group. This one here is believed to be the head of the cell, whereas this other man is actually a registered lobbyist. All the others are employees. Edward is thought to be a small-time player or maybe just an employee hired to deliver messages."

"With the addition of Edward, it looks as if we have the unbroken connection between the terrorist cell and our Mr. Brown, whom they believe to be the spy they hired to infiltrate the aircraft manufacturer." She gestured toward Hal Brown.

Everyone nodded.

"I think we should hear from Sally as to just what this Edward person did," said Bell.

Caroline looked at Sally. "Yes, please tell us," she said.

All eyes turned toward Sally. Without hesitation she relayed the story of how, for months they had her scouting the first-class passengers on those special flights, until one day they told her they had selected Mr. Brown and she would now be promoted to Brown's contact.

Hal broke in, "My job would be long term. They would help me write a code that could be hidden in the millions of lines of code which will control the new autopilot ACAS system. We knew it would take a long time and be difficult, but the hope was that this worm could remain hidden for years until the plane was operational.

"And then a terrorist with the right commands and an SDR could activate the worm and bring down a plane.

"SDR stands for Software Defined Radio. Put in layman's terms this radio could broadcast commands that would interfere with the planes ACAS system," Hal added.

Sally was looking at Hal open-mouthed.

"Understand this system could take years, and maybe wouldn't work at all. It is basically a harebrained idea, but... who knows?" asked Hal.

"I'm just glad they recruited a crack FBI agent," said Caroline.

"Well, thanks, but we don't know who else they have recruited," said Hal.

"And now we know that they had more than one plot going," said Mason.

"Supposing that we arrest these people. What laws have they broken?"

"John, you're the lawyer," said Caroline, looking to her assistant for an answer.

"Oh my, yes, Title 18 allows twenty years in prison for conspiracy to destroy an airplane."

"That's true, but has the law caught up with 21st Century methods?"

"Good question. You're right that most of the laws involve explosives, guns, bombs and so on. I don't believe it speaks specifically about destroying an airplane with software."

There was tittering around the table.

"Like maybe somebody is going to throw software at an airplane."

"Well, I think the last paragraph, number seven is thrown in there to cover everything else not mentioned above," John explained. "Like it prohibits communicating information, knowing the information to be false and under circumstances in which such information may reasonably be believed to endanger the safety of any such aircraft in flight."

"Doesn't it say anything about interfering with an airplane's controls or software?"

"Mostly about bombs."

"Boy, oh boy, we need to update those laws."

"Yup, and when are you planning to run for Congress?" quipped Mason.

Everyone laughed.

"Well, for now, until it expires, we can do a lot of snooping. Most of these conspirators have been caught by snooping into their emails and bank records."

"I think we have already gathered a lot of evidence that way," said Shapiro. "That's how we became suspicious of this lobbying outfit, in the first place. Of course, the terrorists have gotten a lot smarter about that, too. I mean they have lawyers on the staff who study how we have caught people before by watching what they say on emails. And so, they are a lot more careful about what they say, where and how they say it. Nothing beats real evidence, good old face to face testimony and tape recordings."

"Tape recordings?"

"Wire taps."

Everybody looked at Hal.

"Yes, I've recorded my contacts so far," said Hal.

Sally gasped.

"Yeah, I was wearing a wire when we talked," Hal admitted glancing at Sally.

Sally blanched.

Everyone looked at Sally.

"And you?" asked Caroline. "Have you recorded your meetings with Edward and the teenage girl?"

Sally shook her head, horrified.

"How about pictures? Smart phone records?"

"No, nothing," Sally bowed her head.

"How are we going to prove that Sally was operating under instructions from the Lobby Cell?"

"My paychecks from them, maybe?" offered Sally.

"Did you keep copies?"

"No."

"No problem. We can examine the bank records."

"Is that enough?"

"We'll need more proof that Sally actually gets her orders from Edward, who gets them from the Lobby Cell."

Everyone nodded.

Sally started to tremble and feel faint. She lowered her head on the table.

"I'll help you," said Hal under his breath as he took her hand under the table. "Hang on, honey. You're going to be all right."

~~~~~

The Usual Table

Later that morning, Sally sat at her usual table at the airport cafeteria where she and Edward met. Sally had been able to get a last-minute assignment on flight 1715 to Dallas. Likewise, Hal had a ticket in first-class. They had rushed to the airport, by helicopter.

Hal explained that he would have a team of FBI undercover agents positioned nearby her table, surrounding her, their cameras ready to capture the encounter from every angle, as well as three audio recording devices planted so as to capture the voices.

Sally had no reason to doubt him, but she had her cell phone ready to record as a backup. Sally looked around nervously, trying to spot the FBI agents. They must be well hidden as everyone was walking by without stopping. Where was Hal? She couldn't see him. Surely he was there somewhere.

Would Edward show up? Sally thought she had his email address, from previous correspondence. It was her only way to contact him. Would the ruse work?

Sally waited, glancing nervously at her watch. Where was he? She struggled to eat something from her plate, the food causing a lump in her throat. Reaching for her water glass, she jumped when a chair scraped.

"Miss Millecan," said Edward.

"Edward!" she exclaimed.

"Keep your voice down, Miss Millecan," he chided her.

"Oh, sorry."

"And now what is so important that you called me away from my job on short notice?"

Sally's mind drew a blank. "W-Well... uh... I thought you would want to know."

"Know what? Your job is to pass messages, nothing more."

"Uh... well, people don't always act the way you expect."

"What do you mean by that?"

Sally was thinking fast, "Well, part of my job before was to get acquainted with the first-class passengers who worked for certain aircraft manufacturers, you know."

Edward raised one eyebrow. "I don't think you were told to go too far."

"Well, it just so happened that this one guy, Harold Brown was very friendly with me, and we... uh... went on some... d-dates, you know?"

"Dates?"

"Well, I've always been told that what I was doing for your company was perfectly legal and honest, totally on the up and up. Well, isn't it?"

"Never mind that. What about Harold Brown?"

"Well, when your company selected him as their target person, it worked out perfectly because we already had a relationship, you know?"

"Actually, I don't know."

Sally fidgeted with the clasp on her handbag. She prayed Hal's recording was working. "What don't you know?"

"I don't know how this information will affect our plans."

"What plans?"

"Our company has plans concerning the aircraft. You don't need to know," he said, haughtily.

"I see. Well, then, if you are in on the plans, that's all I need to know. I mean they trust you, and I trust you. Isn't that right?"

"Yes."

"Somehow I got the impression that you were just a messenger boy, like me."

"Message boy! No way. I am a very important member of the organization. I am in on all the planning."

"Oh," said Sally. "In that case, I guess you have the authority to approve my relationship with Harold."

Edward sputtered. "There will be no 'relationship' as you people in the West call it. You will deliver messages, that is all."

"B-but Edward, there already is a relationship. Harold and I are... in love."

"Nonsense, love is for Hollywood. Forget that silliness."

Sally opened her purse to get out a handful of tissue, taking a second to finger the record button on her telephone. She worked up some real tears and then turned to Edward with brimming eyes. She buried her face in the tissues.

Edward quietly slipped a gun out of his pocket, laid it on the table and covered it with a large handkerchief. He pulled on a pair of slim leather gloves, and glared at Sally. Casually picking up the gun he growled, "You are coming with me, Miss Millecan."

Sally looked up and sniffed.

"Yes madam, this is a gun. Come along quietly or I will shoot."

"You can't do that!" Sally looked around frantically.

"Don't expect your friend Harold to save you, my dear."

Sally gaped at him and turned white. "What have you done with him?"

"No need, my dear. Mr. Brown is one of us. Come along." He grimaced showing his teeth.

Slowly, Sally arose from her chair, hoping her rubbery legs wouldn't give way. Picking up her purse, she stood, gripping her chair with one hand.

"This way, my dear." Edward motioned toward the closest entrance. Sally turned and headed the way she thought he wanted her to go. At one point she hesitated. She felt the gun in her back.

Edward said nothing. From time to time he urged her onward with a jab to her ribs. Where is Hal? Could Edward be telling the truth? Was Hal a traitor? *Dear God, help me.*

They reached an entrance with automatic doors. Edward pushed her through, grabbed her arm and propelled her toward a dark SUV idling at the curb. A man leaped out and opened the back door. Together he and Edward shoved Sally toward the car. Sally stumbled and fell, halfway in. She felt rough hands pick her up and shove her down on the seat. The door slammed shut. She heard more doors open and close and the car took off. *I can't believe this is happening. Dear God.* Sally tried to scream and raise herself up. Hands shoved her down and stuffed a gag into her mouth. She felt her arms being pulled out of their sockets behind her and something snapped. She tugged on her arms. They wouldn't come loose. *Dear God, where are you?* Every nerve in her body was screaming.

Sally tried to move her head so she could see something—anything. Suddenly a black cloth covered her entire face. *Oh God!*

She heard men's voices but couldn't make out any of it. What were they jabbering? Nothing made sense. It was a lot of sounds jumbled together. And then she heard a shrill woman's voice cut through, "Quiet!" Immediately there was silence. Sally could hear the tires humming on the pavement and traffic noise outside. The car stopped. Was it a traffic light? After a minute she heard car-horns honking and engines starting up. They were moving again. She tried to figure out their position. Occasionally it felt like they were turning, as her body swayed one way or the other. Maybe they were going uphill. A ramp, maybe? And then she could hear the car pick up speed. Could be they were on the Beltway. *Oh God.* She fainted.

Sally slammed awake when rough hands pulled on her legs and others shoved her head. Car doors opened and closed. Bodies and feet made sounds. More running footsteps.

"Hold it right there!" screamed a male voice. "FBI! Drop your weapons!" A shot rang out followed by repeating fire. In seconds it was over.

Sally could feel her limp body being dragged by strong arms. "Drop your guns or I'll kill her," screamed a woman's voice.

Raucous laughter. "Go ahead. Kill her. Save us the trouble."

Sally's body fell in a heap. Her head hit the cold hard floor, followed by more shots. Sally's head swam in the silence that followed.

She heard sirens coming from far away and someone kissing her face. "Sally," the man whispered. "Darling, wake up." First the black cloth slipped away and then the gag came out of her mouth. "Ack," she spat and tugged at her wrists and blinked at the lights.

"Bring me the cutters," yelled Hal. In moments he had her hands cut loose and was holding her gently. "Darling are you all right?"

"Where am I?" she rasped.

"I've got you. You're safe. Where does it hurt?"

"My arms, my head," she managed.

With one hand, Hal gently rubbed her arm while he held her with his other. "Are you shot?"

Sally hesitated, "I don't think so. Are you?"

"I'm okay, but one of our guys is down."

"Oh no," Sally started sobbing and Hal cuddled her closer.
"He'll be okay, don't worry."

The sirens drew near. Sally could see now. They were in some kind of parking garage, underground, she thought. She moved her head to look around and then was so horrified at the carnage that she just turned into Hal's arms and sobbed.

~~~~~

A Slight Concussion

A few hours later she lay propped up in her hospital room. She managed a wan smile at Hal, seated beside the bed. He had never left her side all the way through the transport by EMT, the emergency room, the examination, X-ray and MRI.

"You're awake," he smiled at her. "That's good. I'm supposed to keep you awake, but I couldn't do it."

"Oh? What's wrong?"

"You have a slight concussion from hitting your head."

"Oh, is that all?"

"I think you are going to be very sore for a few days. You were starting to go into shock when the EMT's arrived."

Sally sighed and snuggled down. "I feel kind of tired."

"Yeah, me too."

"You could get in bed with me," said Sally.

"Don't tempt me, sweetheart," Hal grinned.

"Oh, I didn't mean that," she said sleepily, and then thought *Maybe I did mean that.*

Sally rolled onto her side and closed her eyes.

"Don't go to sleep," said Hal.

Sally snored softly.

When she awoke, feeling a bit stronger, she and Hal talked over everything that happened.

"The recordings are good," he said. "We have everything we need. And the video is irrefutable."

"That's good," said Sally. "So you can arrest them, now, right?"

"Well, it's too late for most of them."

"Why?" asked Sally, in alarm.

"They're dead," said Hal matter-of-factly.

And then she remembered the shots, crumpled bodies, the blood. Sally shuddered and bit her lip.

"Only two conspirators were upstairs in their offices a man who was in charge and another man who was the registered lobbyist. The woman Kabandha Ghana went down in the parking garage shoot-out. We got 'em all, Sally. You're safe now."

"And what happened to your people? Was anyone hurt?"

"Well, one of the Air Marshals was shot."

"Oh, I'm so sorry," she frowned. "Will he be all right?"

"They took him right into surgery. It was touch and go for a while, but this hospital is amazing. They can do wonders."

"Yes that's true."

"He'll be okay, but he'll be on the shelf for a while."

"Oh."

"He asked about you," said Hal.

"He did?"

"Yeah, he was concerned about everybody. Nice guy, considering he almost gave his life for you."

"I must do something for him," said Sally, starting to tear up again.

Hal didn't want to upset her. Her emotions were raw right now. She needed rest. Should he say more? Yes, if it was cheerful.

"I think everybody survived and we'll all get a commendation and maybe a bonus. Would you like that?" he asked.

Sally nodded.

"Mr. Goodrich was asking what your last name was, but none of the fellows knew."

"Mr. Goodrich?"

"Nate Goodrich the Air Marshal who helped us rescue you."

"The one who was shot?"

"Yeah, that's the guy."

"Maybe I can do something, send some flowers or something." Sally searched for an idea.

"I think he would be willing to meet you, if you are interested."

"Sure."

"I'll check if he can have visitors and maybe wheel you up later, before his family arrives from the West Coast. Okay?"

"I'd like that."

"Okay, why don't you take a nap now?"

Sally sighed and closed her eyes.

Thank you, God.

Epilogue

$\mathcal{N}$ate was half-way propped up in his hospital bed, his chest wrapped in bandages. An IV ran from the rack into his arm. A nurse hooked up something and fiddled with the controls. Satisfied she dropped her hands, "Can I get you anything, Mr. Goodrich?" she asked. "Raise or lower your bed? Get you some water?"

"Yes, please, water."

She held an iced drink for him, while he sucked on the straw.

"Thanks," he said and looked away.

"You have visitors, Mr. Goodrich. Do you feel up to seeing them?"

"Is my family here?"

"Not yet. They're on their way. It may be tomorrow."

"Who is it?"

"A Mr. Brown and a woman in a wheel chair."

"I don't know them."

"I think you may want to see them."

"Okay, just for a minute. You can raise me up a little for now," said Nate, weakly.

The nurse left the room. She gestured to Hal to come in.

Hal pushed Sally's wheel chair into the room. "Hello, Nate. Remember me? Harold Brown Jr., FBI."

"Oh yeah, one of *them*," Nate tried to chuckle, and it came out more of a choke.

Hal laughed, "Call me Hal, okay? Look here, I've brought someone to see you."

Nate noticed her for the first time. "Well, lucky me, a beautiful woman."

"Not just any beautiful woman. She wants to say something."

"Hi Agent Goodrich. I'm the woman whose life you saved and I'm forever grateful. I just want to say thank you for saving my life." She started to puddle up.

Nate held out his hand. "Come closer, young lady. I'm kind of tied up, here."

Hal wheeled her up to the bedside. Sally put her small hand in Nate's and gazed at him. "Thank you," she whispered, letting the tears fall.

"You are so welcome." Nate studied her for a full minute. "You remind me a lot of someone I used to know," he said quietly.

"I hope that's good," said Sally recovering a bit.

"Oh yes, it was someone I loved, but she's gone now."

"I'm sorry."

"It's all right. She was my first wife who died twenty years ago. My second wife, Nan, and my family will be here tomorrow. They're probably coming in on a red-eye." He sounded tired.

"I don't want to tire you," said Sally.

"I'm okay, for now. I have a boy nineteen and a girl sixteen, going on thirty," Nate tried to joke.

"Wonderful," said Sally, "and their names?"

"Rob, stands for Robert, and Joy Alice. I love them so much."

"That's nice," said Sally not knowing what else to say. "My middle name is Alice, too."

"I guess I don't know your name," said Nate.

"It's Sally Alice."

"Sally Alice. Is that all?"

Sally looked at Hal, in question. "Should I tell him?"

"Up to you," said Hal.

"It's Miller, Sally Alice Miller."

Nate gasped and turned even paler than he was already. Could it be?

"Miller? Are you sure?"

Sally realized she had blurted out her real name, by mistake. Hal looked as shocked as Nate. She tried to recover. "Oh I shouldn't have said that. Uh, please. Oh … please, don't tell anyone," she pleaded. "I go by Millecan professionally. My real name is a secret." She sent Hal an apologetic look.

Nate reached for the bed controls and raised himself up as far as he could. He reached for her other hand. Sally took it and bent toward him. "Look at me," said Nate, gazing directly into her eyes. "I need to ask you a personal question, all right?"

"Okay, you can ask. I don't have to answer."

"This is very important to me," said Nate. "I'm going to guess your age and birthday, and I want you to tell me if I'm right. That's all. Can you do that?"

Sally thought this was very strange. "Maybe."

"You were twenty-one on your last birthday which was just seven days ago."

Sally gasped, "How did you know?"

"Well, I swear this is true, I was there when you were born."

Sally's eye flew wide. "You were? Oh my goodness. I've looked all my life for someone like you. You know who I am!"

"I think that I do, Sally." He squeezed her hands tightly.

They gazed at each other, lost in thought unaware of the world around them.

"Nate, I need to know. Please tell me who I am?"

"Honey, I'm not sure how much of this you can take in, all at once. It's a long story."

"Well, I know my mother, but she refuses to tell me anything about my father or why she changed our name and took me to Canada."

"Probably we can spend some time comparing notes, later. Right now, I think we are both kind of gob-smacked." He looked at Hal for confirmation.

Hal nodded. "Maybe I should take her back to her room and let you both get some rest."

"I know. But, let me just say, I've looked for her for twenty-one years. I don't want to lose her again."

"How's that?"

"My baby girl was kidnapped by her surrogate mother–Ferrell Miller."

Sally released his hands and raised herself, "Who *are* you?" she demanded.

"Sally Alice Miller," said Nate solemnly, "I'm your father." Nate, gulped, tears streaming down his face.

"Oh my God" she said and stared at him searching his face for clues.

Thinking better of it, she asked, "How tall are you?"

"I'm six foot three," said Nate.

"Where was I born?"

"You were born at 7:59 PM, on the 19th, in Portland, Oregon, delivered by Dr. Yarnoka."

"Oh my God. It's true!" She plopped back in her chair and started rubbing her tears away. *Oh dear God, thank you.*

Hal moved up beside them, nearly speechless, himself. "Well," he finally managed, "this is wonderful!"

They both nodded vigorously and smiled through the tears.

"Um... Mr. Goodrich, may I call you Nate?" asked Hal.

"You have to ask?" said Nate, with implication in his words.

"Um, I'm wondering, sir, if it would be appropriate to ask for your permission... uh... to court your daughter?"

Nate looked at Sally who nodded yes.

"It is with the greatest of pleasure that I give my blessing," Nate took Hal's hand. "You've done a good job already, it seems." Nate lowered his bed and half closed his eyes.

"I'd better wheel you back, girlfriend," said Hal.

"But, I don't want to leave," she protested.

"I think you both need a nap."

"I'm too excited to sleep."

"Yes, but didn't you see the sleeping medication the nurse injected into his IV?"

"Bring her back for dinner, Hal. I want to celebrate," said Nate sleepily and closed his eyes.

The End

Author's Notes

Air Traffic Control Systems of the Future

By 2020, the FAA mandates that all planes "announce" where they are as part of the Next Generation system called ADS-B (Automatic Surveillance System- Broadcast). Via the GPS, many commercial airplanes already have the system in place. The altitude, speed and location of the plane is broadcast automatically to relatively inexpensive receiving stations positioned all over. This is especially advantageous for airplanes flying over wide open water, where radar units do not reach. This new system is much faster and cheaper that the old radar systems.

Supposedly, any receiver can pick this up. We posited that the fictitious character, Kabandha Ghana, had an app on her smart phone that could tell her all the planes flying overhead.

Also, most commercial planes now have TCAS, which broadcasts to any plane in the vicinity. Special onboard displays warn the pilot of the danger of a collision and can say, Pull Up, Pull Up, or Descend, Descend and then Level Off when the danger is past.

But, even that is subject to mistakes, because it depends on the pilot hearing the advisory and taking action. And so a very few of the largest trans-atlantic super planes now have the TCAS programmed into the autopilot, so it will automatically take over flying the plane in the case of an imminent threat of collision.

In this fictional story, Kabandha "knew" that experiments were underway to link the ADS-B with the next version of automated Traffic Collision Avoidance System (TCAS), which is already on planes and which can be made to think another plane is in the air next to it already. In this story, the terrorists were after a version of TCAS that integrated ADS-B into it. The person would try to crash the plane using a "Software Defined Radio" (SDR for short) to broadcast these messages.

For our peace of mind, let us presume that the designers of the next system are actually well aware of any such glitches and have designed multiple safeguards against any "worm" entering the system.

Characters and Relationships

Just one of our characters is named after a real living person. Mr. Christopher Wray is the current head of the FBI and was inducted into that post on September 28, 2017. His picture and bio are available online.

All other characters in this book are a product of the author's imagination and have no relationship to any living persons, living or dead except for Caroline Douglas, the "Executive Assistant Director," whose name I borrowed from a couple people.

The special fictional heroine of Ms. Caroline Douglas was created to honor the very few women who have risen to high ranks in the FBI. The name Caroline Douglas actually was my grandmother's name, and so I used the name, as a little tribute to her. The similarity is in name only, as I never knew this grandmother.

Also, among those women who rose to high posts in the FBI were Ms. Stephanie Douglas (no relation) who was the actual head (Executive Assistant Director) of the FBI's National Security Branch, appointed in 2012 where she served until her retirement in 2013.

According to the NY Times, as of 2016 women only held 12 percent of the FBI's 220 senior agent positions, including nine who run field offices. Janice K. Fedarcyk, now retired, ran the New York office, with about 2,000 employees, from 2010 to 2012.

Twenty percent of the FBI agents are women, (about 2700), but no women were agents, at all, until after J. Edgar Hoover's death in 1972.

Hopefully, in the future, more young women will be encouraged to join the scientific community studying computer software technology, perhaps following the model of Amy Hess who is the admired first woman to be head of the FBI's science and technology branch with 6,000 employees.

We believe that women, in general, are subtly discouraged from seeking higher positions in the FBI because of the harsh necessity of moving agents from bureau to bureau at a moment's notice. Difficult as this is for married men, in my opinion, it is even worse for women with children at home.

The Confusing Federal Hierarchy

With apologies and a salute to the current Secretary for the Department of Homeland Security who also happens to be a woman, Ms. Kirstjen Nielsen, who was nominated to that post on October 12, 2017:-

The DHS is in charge of the TSA which is in charge of the FAMS, and not the FBI.

The FBI is really under the Justice Department, not the DHS, however, for this story, we have assumed that they cooperate, at times.

And finally, the Federal Air Marshal Service is a different law enforcement agency from the Federal Marshal Service. Confusing, isn't it?

No Worries

While the titles, posts, cities, countries, airlines and schedules are real, the people and their relationships are totally the author's imagination. The method by which the fictional terrorist might "take-down" a passenger airplane was also a product of the author's imagination. We are still enjoying flying safely everywhere in America.

Peace,   DMM

Glossary

FBI = US Federal Bureau of Investigation
FMS = Federal Marshal Service
FAA = Federal Aviation Administration
TSA = Transportation Security Administration
DHS = Department of Homeland Security
FAMS = Federal Air Marshal Service
DC = District of Columbia
DFW = Dallas/Fort Worth International Airport
SEA TAC = Seattle/Tacoma International Airport
DCA = Ronald Reagan National Airport
YVR = Vancouver, British Columbia, Canada, International Airport
YYJ = Victoria, British Columbia, Canada Airport
LAX = Los Angeles International Airport
IAD = Dulles International Airport
DAL = Dallas Love Field Airport
DCA-SEA = A flight from Reagan to Seattle
TCAS (T'-Kass) = Traffic Control Avoidance System
ACAS (A'Kass) = Air Traffic and Collision Avoidance System
SDR = Software Defined Radio

Cast of Characters

Nate Goodrich
Nan Goodrich
Rob Goodrich
Rob's friends Elvin and Tom
Joy Goodrich
Sally Millecan (Miller)
Mother Ferrell Millecan (Millican) (Miller)
Jeff Totten
Judge Norville Totten. His young wife Mrs. Totten
Sgt. Draff, Police

Officer Sharon McGillicuddy
The teenage girl–Lobbyist contact
George F. George, terrorist alias name
Cabbie
Mavis, Sheldon, Nate's alises
Rosie - desk clerk
Alan Bartle, Hotel manager
Local Cop
Cliff Side, field agent supervisor, Nate's Chicago control
J.Mohammad Mutawassit (meaning moderate, average)
Kabandha Ghana (meaning ugly giant) heads Chicago terrorist cell
Judge Malik Faakhir (meaning master, proud, excellent)
Fadl (meaning reward, favour) Judge's assistant
Danny and Charlie, teen Sunday school boys
Their mother and little sister.
Elder care nurse
Sari - the neighbor snitch
Terry and Rose McGillicuddy
"Papa" Buck Boyles
Justin Lawrence of the law firm of Beetle and Bailey, LLC
Chief Adkins of the Les Plaines PD
Mr. Harold L. "Hal" Brown Jr. Special Agent FBI (bacon and eggs spy)
Daisy, the cat
Captain Mahoney, pilot
FBI Director Christopher A. Wray
Caroline Douglas, FBI National Security Branch. Executive Assistant Director.
John, Caroline's exec asst.
Bell, head of TSA
Shapiro head of FBI Counter-Terrorism
Mason head of Federal Air Marshals

Facts

To overcome some of these limitations, the FAA is developing a new collision avoidance logic based on dynamic programming.

In response to a series of midair collisions involving commercial airliners, <u>Lincoln Laboratory</u> was directed by the Federal Aviation Administration in the 1970s to participate in the development of an onboard collision avoidance system. In its current manifestation, the Traffic Alert and Collision Avoidance System is mandated worldwide on all large aircraft and has significantly improved the safety of air travel, but major changes to the airspace planned over the coming years will require substantial modification to the system.[41]

A set of new systems called ACAS X[42] will use this new logic:

- ACAS Xa will be a direct replacement for TCAS II, using active surveillance
- ACAS Xo will be collision avoidance tuned to work in some currently difficult operational situations, notably closely spaced parallel approaches.
- ACAS Xu will allow multiple sensor inputs and be optimised for unmanned airborne systems.
- ACAS Xp will be designed for aircraft with only passive surveillance (ADS-B).
- The first FAA-scheduled industry meeting was held in October 2011 in Washington DC, to brief avionics manufacturers on the development plans for "ACAS X" - including flight demonstrations scheduled for fiscal

2013. The FAA says its work "will be foundational to the development of minimum operational performance standards" for ACAS X by standards developer RTCA.[43]

- It is estimated that, if ACAS X will be further developed and certified, ACAS X will not be commercially available before mid 2020s. And it is said to be unclear at this stage whether ACAS X would provide any horizontal resolutions.[44]

Stephanie Douglas [now retired] was named executive assistant director of the FBI's National Security Branch by agency director Robert Mueller, on Oct. 3, 2012. Before her appointment Ms. Douglas had most recently served as special agent in charge of the San Francisco Division.

The National Security Branch of the FBI, a very important post, which Ms. Douglas held, is responsible for protecting the U.S. from weapons of mass destruction, terrorism and foreign espionage. It combines counterterrorism, counterintelligence, weapons of mass destruction, and intelligence elements under the leadership of a senior bureau official. It also houses the Terrorist Screening Center, that maintains the Terrorist Screening Database (TSDB), that contains information about all known or suspected terrorists. A number of different government agencies, including federal, state, local and tribal law enforcement agencies, the US State Department, the Bureau of Citizenship and Immigration Services and the Transportation Security Administration use the resource.

The Federal Air Marshal Service (FAMS) is a United States federal law enforcement agency under the supervision of the Transportation Security Administration (TSA) of the United States Department of Homeland Security (DHS).

BOOKS FROM MERCERPUBLICATIONS

Links to all of these books can be found at
www.mercerpublications.com

- **The McBride Series of Action Novels, Starring Det. Lt. Michael J. McBride Jr. available in English and Spanish, ebook, print and Audible editions**

"Car oo6 Responding"
"The Cocaine Chase"
"The Golden Coin"
"The Cartel Wars"
"The Gang Bust"
"Unidad oo6 Respondiendo"
"La Casa di la Cocaina"
"El Immigrant e la Monada Dorada
"La Guerras Cartel"
"La Pandilla Busto"

- **The Washington McBride Novels, Starring Senator Mike McBride, his wife Juliette, featuring his bodyguard, Cynthia Patterson. available in ebook, print and Audible editions**

"the Fairfax Fix"
"the Arlington Alias"
"the Savage Surrogate"

- **The McBride Romances, available in ebook, print and Audible editions**

"Fran and Max" The Bungalow
"Cynthia and Dan," Cyber War
"Mary Beth and Sammy," Rolling Thunder
"Nate" The Search (A Father's Search for His Long-Lost Daughter)

- ### Photo Travel books by Dorothy May Mercer, and Dave Mercer

"Alaska and Back" With Dave and Dorothy, a travel journal.
"Africa and Back" With Dave and Dorothy
"Hawaii and Back, Vol. I Kauai" With Dave and Dorothy
"Hawaii and Back, Vol II, Maui," With Dave and Dorothy
"Hawaii and Back, Vol III, Oahu," With Dave and Dorothy
"Hawaii and Back, Vol IV, Kuai Via S'FO," With Dave and Dorothy
"Niagara and Back," With Dave and Dorothy

- ### Historical books by Dorothy May Mercer:

"Leon and Esther," an historical Christian love story.
"Stories I Haven't Told," an auto-biography

- ### Collections and Miscelaneous Books edited and published by Dorothy May Mercer and Mercer Publications & Ministries, Inc.:

"Let's Talk," a Black/White Dialog in the US and the UK, Various Authors
"He Called Her Hat," That Tough Little Lady, by Myron C. McDonald
"Short & Fun Stories," Vol. 1
"Short & Fun Stories," Vol. 2

- ### The "How to For You" series of booklets for aspiring writers.

How to Write Great Dialog
How to Write Fiction
How to Design and Format Your Paragraphs
How to Write Sentences and Paragraphs in Your Novel
How to Fix Errors in Your Document
How to Format Your Book, for Publishing
How to Sell Your eBook Using Amazon Free Days
How to Add an Interactive Table of Contents
How to Install a Link in Your Document

How to Edit a Book, With a Friend
How to Prepare Your Book for Kindle
How to Use Your Book for Free Ads
How to Design a Kindle eBook Cover
How to Install Your Kindle Cover on Createspace, and Vice Versa
How to Register ISBNs and Copyrights
How to Market Your Book
How to Get an Audible Version, of Your Book
How to Self-Publish

www.ingramcontent.com/pod-product-compliance
Lightning Source LLC
Chambersburg PA
CBHW071005280626
47160CB00015B/1397